Hélène

Pierre Jean Jouve

Hélène

Translated by Lydia Davis

THE MARLBORO PRESS/NORTHWESTERN
EVANSTON, ILLINOIS

The Marlboro Press/Northwestern
Northwestern University Press
Evanston, Illinois 60208-4210

The costs of translation have been met in part by a subvention from the
French Ministry of Culture.

Printed in the United States of America

ISBN 0-8101-6003-X

Library of Congress Cataloging-in-Publication Data

Jouve, Pierre Jean, 1887–
    [Dans les années profondes. English]
    Hélène / Pierre Jean Jouve ; translated by Lydia Davis.
    p. cm.
    ISBN 0-8101-6003-X (pbk. : alk. paper)
    I. Davis, Lydia. II. Title
    PQ2619.O78D3613 1995
    843'.912—dc20   95-37379
                                              CIP

Hélène

I

There is something mysterious and inexhaustible in the relationship among these regions. There is a quality about it that never comes to an end. There are several tiered regions, enclosed in the hundred blue valleys of the hollowed mountains or, by contrast, seated upon the pedestal of rock, light, and abstraction far above. Between those higher places, like the sills of heaven, where glacial masses and scaly tips stand at the edge of a landscape gaunt and happy—and the lands of Italy swollen with lakes, trees, majestic painted churches—the traveller climbs and descends and always rediscovers the same mountain pastures and sanctuaries. Up there he is close to the larches, he looks at the silvery rock with its classical line, and at the green waters within the immense expanse: he believes, if to this his spirit is entirely favorable, that he feels the spirit of God immanent in such objects; here, there are the accumulations of verdure and the troubled dreams of life, the sense of sin, in villages and in churches, and the superstitious spirit of redemption showing through the piety of the people.

I was going to leave this paradise that same day. I was going to leave the valley of the Bondasca with its fresh and dreamy forms, my soul full of the poetry of my sixteenth year, for other countries more ordinary, less dangerous, and I saw beyond the splay of heavy forested mountains the five or six jagged, platinum-colored peaks that dominate the whole of the valley: how much time would go by before I saw them again? Did not the massif itself lie under a strange sign, bearing as it did the name of *Disgrazia*? Walking, I had reached the village of Sogno, which on a sort of amorous green balcony looks out toward those towering misfortunes. So keen were the perceptions of my heart that I felt the suffering of the flowers. The summer was at its height, no wind, and the distant torrent in the lower part of the valley gleamed like an old saber: I sensed the vast expanse of land I had before my eyes as a splendid land of the dead. I saw then I was leaning my back against the roughcast wall of a cottage with one narrow barred window, low-lying in the meadow; the dense grass, thick as a mop, a mane of hair, coiled gently against the stone, and between the sun-scorched wall, the dissheveled grass, and the abandoned window there was such secrecy that I felt moved to tears. The whole of nature, it seemed to me, its past and its future, was summed up on the bright wall of the cottage, just as one had but to enlarge or reduce the cottage in time to obtain the whole of nature, with its happiness and its death: and it was only then that I noticed that the cottage, embedded in a wall, was part of the cemetery. In the shadow of the white campanile, I wanted to go into the cemetery by way of the wormeaten door. The cemetery was a terrace laid out above the natural terrace

2

of the village, a terrace in strong sunlight, with its low wall which appeared against the abyss, and opposite, and higher up, and in the sky, all the wicked peaks of the *Disgrazia*! If I could have spent my life in the lightest of cottages! But inside this cemetery, I was surprised to see no tombs. Unlike the other so Italian cemeteries in the valley, it was formed of grass, that is all, a grass beneath which there were no swellings. As I stepped forward, however, my foot bumped against a tilted iron plaque that bore a number. In Sogno this was a tomb, so very humble, and I imagined the register, kept in the church, in which names and histories were recorded opposite the numbers. The plaque I had stumbled upon was number 37—the figure standing for man, and the figure standing for woman. And I became lost in conjectures but "followed" the rod that from this poor rusted plaque must descend straight to the heart of the mortal remains, man or woman.

I was deeply struck and repeated the number 37 to myself as I left the cemetery. I inscribed my name, LÉONIDE, on the wall with the tip of my pocket-knife so that this wall in bearing my name would eternalize a solemn moment. Then I stepped over the wall and found myself in the large field outside the village. This, at noontime, was a painted landscape, a veritable picture, these enclosures of gray stones, the green dotted with flowers, and the snows sparkling in the background. I had a great feeling of culpability, in the field. I walked, it seemed to me, with my head bowed. I was also warm. I felt a warm, tender breath on my face, like the emanation from some flesh. I gazed off toward "the back," where the rising landscape disappeared, a spot I would reach in half or three quarters of an hour and from which I would have to return. In fact the breeze was as fragrant as flesh, and insistent; it also had the sweetish color of my abandonment.

But why was I speaking of abandonment?—Yes, it was indeed at that moment that the dazzling phenomenon occurred, and only later was I to realize that the idea of abandonment and the apparition followed immediately one upon the other. I first saw the parasol as a changing orb, somewhat yellow and somewhat pink. I caught sight of the spot on the iridescent, melancholy velvet of the fields. Right away I trembled from head to foot. After a bit of hesitation the form appeared to separate itself from the substance of the landscape and to inhabit it: a lady, dressed in light muslin, bare-headed, who held up the train of her dress as she walked. Long gloves clasped the skin of her arms. Her dress was as full as a cloud. Her limbs and her gait seemed to me of a Grecian beauty. Her chest was rising because she was climbing the slope. There were so many attractive parts about her that I could not distinguish her face; or rather I saw her face and at the time did not find anything particular in it. Oval and tranquil. No, the extraordinary thing was what surmounted her face; she had a mass, an edifice of hair; a head of hair, a *chevelure*, at once full, like a nest of snakes, and frothy or radiant like sunlight; whose color glimmered between violet, blond, and a dull red, and in its whole was of an indefinable, warm tone of ash. This *chevelure*, just like the Wonder to Come, was yet unknown to me; I had never seen it; I did not think it could exist. The young woman was walking slowly. No doubt, in her statue-like beauty, she felt only indifference for a stranger's gaze. I was in fact very small within the landscape and she must not even have seen me. Yes, she was extremely beautiful with a statue's beauty and she knew how beautiful she was. She was drawing near. She was going to come along the path where I was.

I detected in this creature, so extraordinary (because of her beauty, because of her dress, amidst these mountain pastures), the strangest sort of disharmony. On the one hand a tranquillity of body and movement that one associates with plants, on the other hand a hidden and quite violent fire—a fire burning I didn't know where, in her body or in some parts of her body, like her *chevelure*. Her character was proud, but was it not in the spirit that she bore this fire, a dark fire, whose burning was almost vulgar? It was no doubt the idea of this fire, this feminine fire, that impressed me, and to such a degree that in the Sogno meadow that day, before the stranger in the white dress, it was as though I felt myself as a woman, and felt drawn to her in that way. Yes, in effect, feeling a little like a woman, I understood a beautiful woman. Never had I so well experienced the approach of a woman as I did now, when the White Form was advancing to meet me. She was walking with small steps towards me. She was barely lifting her high heels in the grass or on the pebbles of the path, but her body, so simple, showed to such advantage that I thought I was seeing a dance rather than a walk. —For I must say something of the difficulty I had with women.

I was a big boy by then, and well built. I felt independent, but I was unsociable, and I affected a severe man-

5

ner. With regard to women, I was full of politeness and
deference; but deep down (quite to the contrary) I
wanted to strike them. My fear of their presence, of their
smell, was extreme, as was my hatred of their smooth and
velvety skin. It would also happen that, before the teas-
ings of certain friends of my mother, emotion would seize
my chest and cause my heart to beat faster and faster and
more and more heavily: I would feel everything getting
out of hand. I gave women the impression that I was
observing them with spite, and their hostility recom-
pensed my need, always repressed, for their tenderness.
But it went *altogether otherwise* with the stranger in the
meadow: at first, I felt light-hearted and young; I experienced an unaccustomed easing of my hatreds. I was
abruptly overcome with pleasure at the beauty of things,
of the high, fertile plateau, of the rocks of the Bondasca
and the columns of clouds, of Sogno under its splendid
erect white campanile. I noticed my own erotic state,
then. Finally the beauty, the harmony, the rising up of the
world, ended in an illumination that revealed to me, as
the cause of all this, shining like a saint's halo, through
the wind and the heat, formed of a substance either silver
or black or violet: that *chevelure*.

For a moment my fingers toyed with the visor of my
cap and availed themselves of those long instants with
anguish; I was little by little preparing what I wanted to
do and what was intended to express the storm of my
passionate feeling. I wanted an act, I would have it. My
fingers took hold of the blue edge of the cap, my arm felt
how it was going to curve and unbend. The trembling
(for I was trembling) had localized in those legs become

useless. The figure came close to me at last. My fingers seized the cap, and slowly, majestically, with my arm curved, I bowed to her.

The *chevelure* inclined. She was answering me.

The significance of her body! She laughed and I glimpsed her teeth.

II

I was in an utter daze when I arrived at the restaurant, but without being moved to find out what had happened or to learn anything about the stranger. I was savoring my giddiness.

Sitting at my table I ate as though in a dream; at the next table, however, favorably seated in the room according to the custom of the country, were three priests. While in the midst of my curious state my eyes were fixed on them. One was surely the curé of Sogno, that fat one with a glass eye; the second a young village curate; but the third, a very carefully kempt clergyman, come from a distant town, presented singular characteristics of which I became little by little aware, for his face was powdered and, it seemed to me, his lips painted; and this one was looking at me with a sustained attention that had a disturbing effect on me. All three were talking about the same person: the Countess Hélène de Sannis. Despite myself I learned some things about this person and her family (the rouged priest was a glib speaker). I heard that the Sannis family occupied the foremost place in the armorial of the province, in both the highlands and the low; that while the Château de Ponte, in the valley, was the most important (the whole Sannis line stemmed from there), the Cas'alta or summer house in Sogno had grace and charm; but that the list had to include another two or three massive dwellings, readily recognizable by the majesty of their gates, in the villages of the upper regions, belonging either to them or to their relatives by marriage, all of this forming the patrimony on which they based their very Christian power; and that by means of this great development of riches and virtues, through fair times and evil the Sannises had led the country, spreading good around them, and holding their own against the Bondos, their enemies, or rather their honorable rivals, for a good half-dozen centuries. The priest with the painted lips was looking at me in a manner still stranger as he described the *Contessa Elena a'Sannis*: "She is no longer very young, but one must agree that she has truly extraordinary hair."

My mind was made up: I would get away away from there. Very quickly, I stood up, paid, and went out. The afternoon was splendid, as though varnished beneath the light. Farewell, Sogno! I set off at a run, *I fled*, quite determined to catch the four o'clock mail-coach in the valley. But I wanted to have another look at Torre, which is a wonderful place because it is so wild, a place in which I had spent such lovely hours the week before, at a time when nothing had yet happened of what was now overwhelming me (I was thinking of the woman of the meadow, whom I was calling Hélène). I was hurrying down through woods of young beeches, chestnuts; it was

hot; sweat beaded on my forehead and around my neck
and behind my ears; I flushed a viper that disappeared in
a rustle of dry leaves. As in my inner sight the beautiful
white woman's outstanding features began to fade I became submerged by sadness. Here was Torre. And what
did the apparition of that horrible rouged priest signify?
What did he want with me? And why had he for so long
(the entire duration of the meal) trotted out his dubious
anecdotes about *Hélène de Sannis*, trying to make *me*
believe that this woman was the one I had encountered
and greeted that same morning?

At Torre the effect is of solemnity. A small Roman
church in ruins and a farm, solitude. What I had been
taken by at Torre was not only the woods pierced with
spots of sunlight, the mass of melancholy foliage, distant
villages of colored stone, waterfalls, springs; it was also
people, a man and several women; the man, the father,
the women, his daughters. I was not long in finding them
again where they were, tending the vegetables. The Father, bare above the waist, his chest jutting beneath his
swarthy skin, covered with black hair, his feet bare in the
loose soil, he had appeared to me the most darkly beautiful man in the village: and thus he was now, with his
John the Baptist's bearded face, and he bent down and
straightened up again, tossing something to his oldest
daughter, who was standing laughing and with her bare
muscular legs wide apart on the soil, who was holding out
her apron and caught the thing against her belly; and the
other girls around them watched their Father with a sup-
pressed merriment, and when they took their eyes away
from him hoed the earth in front of him; and the young-

est (a simpleton), sitting directly on the warm earth, rocked from one thigh to the other, for the Father. The same scene that I had already witnessed. The first time, these poor folk in the landscape of Torre had reminded me of the Bible, of Lot and his daughters, of the troubled and sacred Family, and I had said to myself that this man and these women possessed the secret of a monstrous happiness. It was therefore this that I had wanted to see again—in coming back here; but why had I wanted to see them again just after seeing Her of that morning? Why this relationship or this superimposition? Yes, they were beautiful, not guilty, almost ritual. Certainly John the Baptist was sleeping with his daughters, at least the oldest daughter, and as with all sacrilegious things about such a love there was a particularly brilliant aspect, whose gleam overspread the beauty of the evening in that god-fearing and poor and roadless place where the tall palms gave shelter to profound need and convenience. But affected, no doubt, by "something else," I could not recapture my real interest in them, my admiration, I now viewed them somewhat as though they were animals. The little simpleton caught sight of me and came up and danced around me: she unendingly repeated the same frightful gesture under her skirt; they recognized me for they had once offered me a light repast in their house. The father stopped working, and showing his white teeth he brought out a few strident words (whose meaning was scarcely comprehensible to me). The daughters were sweating; they passed their two bare forearms, one after the other, over their damp hair; the odor was indeed that of animals.

I said to them that I was about to leave. They did not understand but they wanted to give me something to drink inside the farmhouse. No, I said, I'm leaving. By then my distress was extreme. I lifted my hand to say goodbye to them.

At that moment the whole tableau was struck by a clap of thunder. Alongside the church, on the rocky path, a superb, simple young woman could be seen in a soft gray costume for walking, wearing small boots, her bare hand resting on a walking-stick. Without recognizing anything of her face, I rediscovered the body (the hips, the shoulders) of the woman in white, and moreover the straw hat she was wearing was unable to contain the masses of her auburn *chevelure*.

Hélène de Sannis! She seemed to be rising from the valley.

I realized that the people of Torre belonged to her, for John the Baptist immediately moved towards her, looking down at the ground, and the three girls, stock-still, darkened like a sky covering over with clouds. The entire family standing about Torre seemed to turn into a group of statues. I was no less a statue, petrified by the surprise of a second encounter in the same day, by repressed excitement, by the intuition of a serious event. A sapphire sky was concentrating all its forces before evening; a hundred thousand leaves (I could have counted them) shone like tongues; everything was odd, stretched out, or condensed, or multiplied, or broken by the light. —I think my mind wandered for a moment. I no longer saw either Torre or the rest of the world, I was no longer there, there or elsewhere, after thinking the phrase "I have seen her twice," which established the limit of human happiness. By the time I emerged from that brief abstraction, the peasants had vanished, the woman was standing next to me.

Her face was pale and lovely. And the *Chevelure*! the tresses of the woman in the sky above the meadow and in all of life.

She gave me a smile of such sweetness that I could not move. She placed her hand, a broad, white, veined hand, on my chest, and she said to me:

"I think you're charming. Do you want to be my friend? Let's go."

Already we were climbing up through the forest.

III

. . . Every day I would betake myself to the meadow, at noon.

I spent the morning preparing. I involved myself with nothing else in order to have my entire freedom, and all my energy for the midday ritual: I visualized nothing for the day other than that unique ceremony. The morning having been employed in constructing by anticipation the circumstances of the solemnity—however brief—, the evening was taken up by the memory, the recollection of its smallest details. One day thus flowed into the next. The clock of time was stopped at *noon*.

I have to say I paid the utmost attention to my appearance. That was for arresting time by means of a charm. Not for her, not to excite her pleasure at seeing me, but in order to seize her in the passage of time I performed meticulous ablutions, I put on clean linen every day, I sought out subtle harmonies, interplays, among the various elements of my costume. It was easy for me to be elegant in order to speak to her imagination, but more difficult to put into effect through my elegance the magical action that was to suspend time.

Hélène de Sannis always appeared in the same spot, between two grassy hillocks. She would be coming from the superb Cas'alta that had been identified for me, higher than the village, but she was far removed from the Cas'alta and from any historic house: a sunflower of a woman in the *full sun* whose dress changed as she moved, a fairy enchantress with an almost divine power hidden in her skirt, and another terrible power formed of tangled, fulvous hair; and I being endowed with a protean range of inward colors, more variable than she perhaps, and feeling myself even the injured child that awaits the Gorgon's gaze. She came from far away. I was ready. Innocently I walked in a different direction from hers, arriving once from the mountain and once from the valley, and if the peasants were observing us they could not think anything amiss. All my carefully calculated movements seemed admirable to me. I saw her, the created one, the creator. At the same time I saw how she had changed, I saw how she was the same. My mind spun. My eyes were full of tears and I laughed with a conquering air. I was incapable, however, of looking critically at what was happening, or even of imagining that I loved her.

And when she arrived in my air—breathable, for my lungs to fill with, it seemed to me—altogether huge and light, but fragrant, above all fragrant—, I put my hand to my cap in a studied gesture, my arm nicely bent, and with a grave, a ritualistic movement, I greeted her.

Once she answered with her celestial smile; another time she inclined her head and said good day to me;

another time she stopped and we walked a few steps together: each step: a world of marvels. Finally, she spoke to me. On one or another of her gifts hung my day, the time of my life, my life. Had she passed without giving me anything, I would have died.

"Good day, Léonide. Are you happy this morning?" (That speech had all its significance, coming from her mouth.) Or: "It is lovely this morning, is it not ravishingly beautiful. We are having the very purest kind of summer." And she added that "Down there it is very hot," holding in her long smooth hand an open letter—and I do not know why the image of the letter engendered in me the image of a husband to whom she belonged. She also asked me if I liked "her mountains" and pointing to the jagged Disgrazia that spread out underneath the empty sky the fascinating desolation of its seracs and its cuirass of snow, she asked me if I had no wish to go there. Whereas my only wish, one that made my soul reel with pleasure, was to be near her—and what did those heights matter to me, apart from their being "her mountains." She also said to me that my cravat was of a very pretty style, that my breeches became me, but into her tone there slipped a silky irony, a faint sarcasm that could also have been a caress, a joy that could have had to it a funereal glimmer: at the same instant, the eyes looking forth under her hair showed a sort of opaqueness and their gaze clouded perceptibly. I did not lose myself trying to penetrate these furtive things; that would have led me in my inexperience straight to secret abysses that I wanted only to touch without knowing them; and in its train it would have brought me "her life," which I did not want to know anything about. I liked our mysteries better. Our mysteries were instantaneous. I attributed to her mysteries a dwelling-place, which was her *Chevelure*— her mysteries of which I had such great need and which enveloped my desire. Ever more beautiful, ever more mysterious, that mass, full of folds and clouds, of blood-red sheens, of black caverns, in which my gaze drowned while experiencing the voluptuous pleasure of death. Everything in the *Chevelure* appeared disturbed, in disorder: the locks, the strands, the hairs thwarted one another, knotted, married, destroyed one another. Here it was a marriage of animals and there a mingling of fumes. The *Chevelure* was a place far vaster than the region of those mountains. "Léonide, are you well this morning?" So ordinary a phrase, but pronounced in a voice of an extraordinary *density*, seemed to me then of the same essence as her formidable hair, and by way of the phrase I entered her hair. Through the phrase I smothered under the smells, the acrid, natural, sexual perfumes, the emanations, the scents, as of an animal. I saw myself surrounded on all sides by those immense and shadowy hairs that were on her more immense, more shadowy than on any other woman's body, and which, with their volutes, their knots, under their iron pins, disclosed the force of her secret and of her being. No! I did not need to be introduced into the real story of her life, to run up against the walls of her marriage, of her social situation. No; I held her, so to speak, against the sky; and there in a continuous exaltation that was accompanied by lively transformations of my sex, I entered into the secrets of the *Chevelure*.

17

"Would you come to the Cas'alta this evening at about five o'clock to have tea? I will be there alone."

And yet the day I heard this amazing sentence I suffered, precisely because of my method of entering into those secrets, which so pleased me; a first consolation was occurring in the substance of my love. I understood that I would have to continue and act, do something now. Torre, with its warm light and the age-old happiness of seeing, had until then illuminated the scene between her and me. Now new movements would be called for, more difficult, less beautiful, and above all unknown to me—because the effect of Torre was ended. I would have to go on; it did not occur to me that perhaps I would have to lose; so far was I from considering the object, envisaging only the splendor of my goal, which was my pleasure in these conditions, pleasure for me, only me, or for the celestial Narcissus. The afternoon of the day on which she said that to me, it began to rain; the countryside became almost invisible, and Sogno was surrounded by phantoms.

IV

While still in the lane, overwhelmed by my audacity, I
felt I must be in the midst of a waking dream, and I no
longer saw the reason for all this.

A woman of the Sannis family! what had this to do
with me, a mere middle class inhabitant of M***? —The
rain dripped down, the gutters of the lofty Cas'alta
spouted cascades on the sharp-pointed pavement of the
middle of the lane. —That awful and ominous din of
water recalled to me the existence of a Colonel de Sannis,
a big man, a great clod, I had been told, who was off on
manoeuvers at this time. My efforts not to perceive this
Comte Humbert de Sannis were futile, since he came to
meet me all around his home. I did not see that there
could ever be any relations between the colonel and me;
besides, I had a loathing for the army: that *instinctive* aversion was in me well before I met Hélène. My scorn for the
military contrived to simplify, so to speak, my problem
with the Comte de Sannis. There is less guilt in having a
connection with the wife of an officer than with any other
married woman, I said to myself as I walked along the

walls of the lane; what is an officer's wife? Treasure belonging to the army, that is to say to everybody.

Such were the curious notions in my mind when I lifted the knocker and rapped at the central door.

I left my damp coat in a very high-ceilinged white-washed room filled with chests. It seemed to me it was cold and even that this cold was sepulchral. I went up a double staircase in stone that led above to three similar doors. The last one on the right having opened, I entered a room that seemed to me *flooded with light*: I was in Hélène de Sannis's parlor. I had at first had that sense of light as I looked at Hélène de Sannis sitting in a high-backed chair near the window, but immediately afterward I had the feeling that it was *very dark*. I struggled between the two impressions. The room was large but very cluttered with ornaments. I preferred to look at the room than to rest my eyes on that almost divine woman who had the goodness to smile at me. While greeting her I went on looking about the insipid room of soft blond wood, in which the panels were divided into coffers of different sizes punctuated by knots that gave a rather crude effect, in which the doors were sunk in thick walls and framed with a triple molding and a thin, very prominent cornice, in which the panels of the doors appeared rectangular but were in fact scalloped with numerous spirals, in which the hardware on the doors was enormous and complicated, like ancient suits of armor. Madame de Sannis appeared to me at last against one of these doors, a very prisoner of the door, framed by the old door's proportions, surrounded by its strange atmosphere—fruit entirely of flesh clothed in a homey fabric.

For a moment, now, she had been speaking and I had been answering her, but probably neither of us had noticed. Was she in a state of emotion, then? I could have known if only my own emotion had not got in the way, but I had no sense either of myself or of her. And while she was pouring the tea I had a vision of Hélène de Sannis: she was the prisoner of a dead beauty, and I was coming to deliver her.

For the first time I experienced the *Chevelure* from close on.

The form, the nuance of the carelessly gathered, heaped up, twisted coils, all that I had admired and adored until now, only enriched something else, something simpler, and even that madly abnormal purplish-blue tone was only an ingredient. The real virtue was the power of a magnet, exercised by an organ. The real virtue consisted in the magical presence of the *Chevelure*, which acted *as a magnet* to attract one toward hitherto unsuspected joys of the soul, or of the body, of which it was the sign. —Abruptly I had an image of a very red thing in her hair.

I felt a violent shiver, believing I had the thing up against my eyes, seen from very very close. I was gripped by disgust, fear, anguish. An inner earthquake. At that moment Hélène de Sannis turned on the electric light in the room, and a soft and peaceful brightness fell over her hair. What a beautiful head of hair!

I could hardly believe what had happened to me: that vision. It immediately seemed to me old, old, come from the depths of time, but my emotion scarcely subsided under the tender, kind gaze of Madame de Sannis. The first intense disturbance having passed, I nevertheless noticed that Hélène's eyelids were fluttering continually and I took that nervous motion for a sign of acquiescence that, in its anguish, her secret being was addressing to me. Thus, already I was noting what a difference there was between Hélène visible and Hélène concealed, between her and her, between the I of her speech and the I of her features, of her body. Already I saw "her." But then the same must have been true of me; and she saw "me," she so manifestly knowing, I so childish and obscure. Perhaps I was very mistaken in attributing anguish to her? For was she not some twenty years older than I? At any rate, I who was reasoning about the game was fiercely playing the game. Her "Have this little toasted roll" or "Does your cup still have tea in it?" were said with a palpitation underneath, a stirring of womanly heat, lips half open and secretly so (the red thing?), words she released without owning to them, that she regulated perfectly since her aim was to use them (without owning to them), that I registered as not owned to, and that I did not know how to use, that I wanted to go on provoking again and again, more and more. Even an idiot knows how to manage love. Our game of blind-man's bluff became such that we began to talk about all sorts of pointless subjects, the weather, fashion, walks in the mountain, gardens, reading, even marriage, heeding only the second meaning of our words. A wonderful and all but forbidden exchange, which would lead to no consequence. Nothing could remain in that state, but what a pleasure to find oneself in it! No real allusion to a real life, the one surrounding us: only to Life—which moves away from life, which does not exist. "I will introduce you to my sister," she said. "She is much younger than I. She is a girl who is thought to be beautiful, and she is also good. She has very beautiful hair, the same color as mine, but better! You will see." The sister was she herself. I answered that I wished only to become acquainted with her sister Angèle, and that if her sister resembled her, I would feel nothing for her sister but veneration. "It isn't veneration that's wanted, for Angèle!" she said with vivacity, and she burst out laughing. "Gratitude in the place of adoration, then." "Yes, gratitude. Who knows?"

In actuality, the whole of that first afternoon in her house went by in absolute happiness, as though each were singing the praises of the impossible. And it was she, yes it was she who with the maturity of her reason seemed grateful to a child, but it was the child who dove into her, head first, and we no longer knew who had begun, nor what lay in the offing, within vague and menacing Nature.

V

By day, the little valley that could be seen from one of her windows was simple and melancholy. It immediately seemed to me that she had made the valley for herself, that she had chosen it in order to install her window there. A few rocks, a thin stream (very blue when the weather was fair) and no trees, beyond which there were distances as harsh and as suggestive as in Spain, from what I imagined. It was profound, beautiful, and sad. It tugged at one's heartstrings. Hélène de Sannis claimed that this landscape was simply "pretty." Was she always sincere when she spoke? I had doubts—but she was always beautiful, and profound, like the valley. She had chosen that sad spot, whereas the fanfares of the more successful among the mountains resounded all about Sogno and the Cas'alta. By contrast, the private room of Comte Humbert de Sannis looked out over the whole countryside, as did a large rather sinister formal room between the husband's room and the wife's. I looked at Hélène's "boudoir": adjoining the stylish furniture were feminine sorts of chairs, ottomans and bergeres in the worst taste. She appeared to cherish only one thing: a small inlaid Italian armoire that was locked.

While my mind was so happily curled up against her, and her own gazes (moist ones?) were fixed on me, I could not help noticing these particular details around her, and many others, which displayed to me the unknown and the intriguing. There were lots of them; her acts did not square very well with what reason might have called for. She drew me to her home almost every day: did she worry about tongues starting to wag in the neighborhood? I have a strong respect for people's feelings and I might perhaps have wished for a more discreet relationship; nevertheless, her freedom enchanted me. There was in me a subtle mixture of mindlessness and practical thinking. As for her, it seemed that all practical thinking was alien to her, especially where the purpose was of self-preservation.

Nor did I understand her instincts. If I received a letter from my mother, who in her uneasiness was calling me home, she shrugged her shoulders. If I had encountered for the third time the same man occupied in spying on me when I entered the Cas'alta: "That's Bef . . . , I know him well, an emissary from the curé!" she would cry, with joy, and she would burst into laughter, a silvery, heartrending laughter that made me love her hard, *terribly hard.* Impossible to defend myself, impossible to struggle against her. Struggle against whom? On the ceiling, in the middle of a large Greek cross formed by the panels of wood, was carved the coat of arms of the Sannis: first another cross, apparently of rolled up leaves, then a medallion composed of gentian flowers and the same rolled leaves, lastly the crown, and the escutcheon: a small flaming tree on the chief, on the base a grill of four bars.

She looked at me looking at the arms, and the magnificent ceiling, with a spirit of amused lassitude—wasn't there a subtle wickedness in the firm set and moist sheen of her lips? All of this together came to my mind despite me. She was remembering, thinking, and musing. But then her eyes became full of the most voluptuous *dreaming*.

"The golden tree of life is green." I was to learn later what an extraordinary capacity for dreaming she had; and that if her dreaming went back so far, and her dreaming was so directed, if she spent so many hours of her life in golden reveries of closeness, of contact, or of flight, it was because she accepted her trouble, the burying of almost all of the river of her desire beneath the cloak of her splendid frigidity, and because she loved the state she would be in as she opened the sluice-gates of her dreaming. The features of her impassive and passionate face were designed so that she might dream.

I sensed her odd freedom; I thought I understood after some brief allusions that she did not consider herself constrained to faithfulness towards her husband, but under the obligation of obedience. (It is in truth only now that I am able to formulate a proposition: that her woman's nature was adulterous; not in the sense of pleasure: an adulterous woman who had perhaps had no lover but whose heart always dwelled upon *the other*.) If I had been able to perceive this truth in Madame de Sannis's oddly accoutered room, I probably would have fled! —If I had understood this truth, everything would have followed the same course, descended the same slope, and nothing of the fatality would have been deflected: for in sum I did understand this truth. What remained for me to understand was only her "obedience," as it remained for me to come to know M. de Sannis, her husband.

This was no doubt why a tremor of pain, of blame, showed furtively upon Hélène's brow and in her eyes when overly long silences settled between us, which she always tried to break with her smile. She "no longer knew what she was about" and that distraught nobility would strike me (strikes me still) as one of the beautiful things on this earth.

She wore a checkered dress and her mysterious orange perfume. I called her that day "Henrika of the checks" in memory of a certain poem. Or she wore, as a surprise, an entirely black silk dress. The dress, cut rather low, showed as it were a beach of flesh, exceedingly fine in texture: it extended between her two shoulders. A skirt of striped wool, worn with a bolero, hugged her waist tightly and turned it into a "wasp" waist; I fought a war against that skirt. Hélène de Sannis kept changing her dress for me. In turn she played with my cravat, my handkerchief, my woollen or linen vest, and my belt, all the while we talked about music or philosophy. But the day this happened I was truly too close to her, my nostril filled with her real presence, smelling her body, and my eyes fixed upon the foaming of the *Chevelure*; I put my hand into her hair, and was surprised to feel that it was so warm. Hélène returned my kindness with her noblest smile. She also announced to me that her husband was about to return home.

VI

. . . I was invited, I believe, to a wedding, and the wedding ceremony was taking place in the mountains, in that grand manor house on the left. In front of the château, meadows. Small green valleys regularly succeeded other small green valleys in that spot, and the mystery of the place was heightened by the impression given by the arrival of twilight. Everyone is familiar with that sharp, anguished feeling of late autumn evenings in the mountains. Meanwhile I approached the wedding house and I saw the guests arriving, all people related to me. Actually, these were latecomers; the marriage had been celebrated in the morning and the party was in full swing inside; on the threshold of the magnificent building, we saw that the merriment was intense. For my own part I was tormented by the fact of being so late and I was looking for the bride, to whom I had to pay my respects. However some people were expressing doubts about the value of the marriage and going so far as to claim that it would be a "bad marriage." Impossible to see the bride, to make her out in the press of people. Impossible to pick out this woman, though she was very beautiful. But there a movement occurred in the crowd and the bride was before me, for she was parting the people in order to leave. The bride had just changed her outfit and she was wearing an entirely black dress in which her swaying croup stood out very distinctly along with her black hip. I realized that I did not know this woman.

They obviously wanted to prevent the bride from leaving. There were all sorts of stirrings, clearly because of the bad marriage. I too became extremely agitated. The black woman was in the meadow at dusk, beautiful and magnificent. I rushed in all directions, I talked to everyone. I explained that such a bad marriage ought to be stopped by force. I asked Madame N***, my friend, and then Madame V***, to intervene. I begged. The bride was looking at me, however, and I could not be mistaken about the meaning of that look, it was a look of scorn. The bride stretched her arms as though she were sleepy, and the pure and simple truth was, was it not, that she was duty-bound to go join her husband, who had already left, for the honeymoon. It was then I realized that for me the beautiful bride was an object of love.

I "saw" everything, her dreadful fate, her martyrdom. The superb woman was in the meadow, keeping her friends at a distance with her raised arm. She moved a little, more sinuous than a snake, and her teeth illuminated the night. Then was it all over, was there nothing more to be done, for her, for me? But she raised her arm still more forcefully, and she laughed, she uttered a shrill laugh that spread, echoing, through the amphitheater of mountains, and as this despairing laughter burst from her the beautiful woman went off to her death among the green valleys, while our whole scene faded in the green and black mist . . .

VII

I felt that some harrowing event had occurred within me.

Therewith a particular anxiety took hold of me.

Colonel de Sannis was to arrive the next day. I found myself in Hélène's parlor. Madame de Sannis appeared in gay spirits.

In any case, I believed that I viewed the return of Hélène's husband as an altogether natural and *expected* event and I was prepared to find the Comte de Sannis a man worthy of the highest regard and true respect, and one whose esteem I would succeed in winning. Thus, the kind of sorrow that we felt together was entirely dissimulated, and Hélène de Sannis told me the way she had invented to introduce me to her husband: as a young friend of her sister Angèle whom she had met last year at the marriage of the Z***'s. This year, Angèle had had the idea of sending the young man to visit, and they had quickly become fond of one another. The secret part of Hélène had to fight against many impulses to laugh as she told me this fairytale, which she accompanied with all the winks of love. She added that she would, furthermore, be writing to Angèle "should the suspicions of Colonel de Sannis be awakened."

I too began to feel the intoxication of the adventure. This goes far to help one endure, ahead of time, the blows one's happiness will receive. It was impossible to foresee what the Comte de Sannis would be like physically: for Hélène's lips were sealed in his regard. But what I foresaw was a very tall man, very formidable, a fortress of a man (in conformance with the description I had been given at the inn). The intoxication of the adventure was enriched by the intoxication of the lie (the lie seemed to me of an extraordinary value; it created a shared state between us, it isolated *us* from the rest, it already connected us in physical substance) and all of this gave me a perverse pleasure that developed in one direction while being traversed, in another direction, by the great pangs of obscure anxiety I have spoken of.

I remember that afternoon of enchantment, the last free one.

She had said: let us go into the garden. We had descended into the little garden of boxwood, of stone and gravel, rather damp but in full sun, and perfumed with some past or other, and she had sat down on the balustrade, wrapped in a shawl, for the season was advancing. From second to second my emotion grew before her bodily splendor, as did my love—for the golden helmet of her hair, since in the sun that day it was gold—for her remarkably pale skin, for her person, of a grace so melancholy. But she was seized by a whim. She went to get a bowl full of soapsuds, which she set on the balustrade.

Hélène plunged a bit of straw in the soapy water, and then, raising the straw toward the sky, brought it to her mouth. From the straw tube, under the ray of sunlight, emerged a bubble swollen by her breath. A bubble that became bigger and bigger, iridescent and fragile, perfect, reflecting deformed the garden and the sky, a bubble of her breath, which in the end she caused to detach itself and go off through the air. While she was following it with her eyes the bubble burst. She laughed, she smiled, she puckered her lips and blew and sprinkled soapsuds around her. She told me to do the same. Even though I was tempted to put my lips to the straw that was touching her own, I refused: "I prefer to watch," I said, quickly correcting myself with: "I find it more wonderful to watch." Hélène did not tire of bringing forth bubbles. When all the water was used up, the sun withdrew and we went back indoors; my knees were trembling.

In her little parlor, quieted by the subdued light, we sat down. She settled herself in the depths of her bergere, heaving a sigh. She gave one the impression of being on the point of taking flight. In any case, her gaze was directed upon something ever more distant. I could not follow it that far. She was apparently forgetting my presence. As for me, I ran my hand absentmindedly over the beautiful inlaid wood of the little locked cupboard, the one she was so fond of: for a moment now I had been feeling, on the wood's surface, a relief whose design I was following; I saw that my fingers were in this way becoming aware of the form of a letter, no, of two letters: H. H. intertwined in a foliated scroll. H., Hélène. Did her family's name begin with an H? In no way, since the first

letter of her maiden name was P. Then I made up my
mind to understand the meaning of the second H.
Hélène—Humbert (the French form of the name). And
Comte Humbert was going to return home the next day.

*Idiot, I could have opened my eyes to the comedy before
this*, I thought, almost aloud, almost muttering; (and if
someone had asked me: what comedy? I would have had
nothing to say in answer). Without attracting attention I
noted that the two conjugal letters had been added to the
top of the much older piece of furniture, and my teeth
suddenly ground together. Hélène had remained in her
revery—a revery drawn by an artist, a true "woman in
black" revery—and saw nothing of my disturbance,
whereas still touching the two intertwined letters I was
imagining: what will she be doing with him tomorrow
night? And still touching the two letters, I contemplated
the almost too hard form of her breasts in the area of the
nipples, whose location I was able to guess, I noticed that
her legs were majestic, all the way to the depression in her
skirt, where she had laid one hand, and lastly upon the
index finger of that hand I saw a ring shining.

The impressions of irritation, of desire, of despair, and
also an abrupt return of that unilateral happiness, of the
happiness of Torre, the need to seal with a pact something that had taken place within my own self—all this
was impelling me, and as I yielded to this general impul-
sion my distress eased. I had to. It was no longer possible
for me not to perform the whole sequence of automatic,
necessary motions.

As though in the night—as though in a dream—I approached the bergere, I forced myself to go all the way up

to her *body*, which terrified me, before which my head would spin. I had to. I cannot describe the state of irregularly rapid activity my heart was in: the beats merged in a single terrible "Woo-oo" deep in my chest. In my ears it was the noise of the ocean. But I went. The woman of the dream was coming near, then became very near, very near, holding perfectly still. And at first closer than all the rest was her *Chevelure*, magnetic and sexual. I still had myself well enough in hand, within the whirlwind of my senses, within my dizziness and fatigue, to be able to do what I had resolved to do: and slowly, profoundly, I placed my kiss in her hair.

It seemed to me that I was falling so far that there was no removing my lips from her hair.

She did not stir. She consented. She liked it, then. I also felt that she was motherly.

But I had to withdraw my mouth from that world below and above the world, her *Chevelure*, whose substance, smell, and spirit were such that never could I have had any intimation of it if I had not kissed it. I won my mouth away, so to speak, from the temptation of arriving at "divine death" in her *Chevelure* (it was Hélène who used that expression to speak of the kiss) and I jumped back a step, waiting for what she was going to say . . .

I do not know how with her tranquil and tender face she let me know of her "disappointment," but I saw it immediately. I do not know how a sense of her irony, of my inadequacy, of some falling short were conveyed to me. The stinging reaction to failure took place underneath, despite the amorous demeanor I preserved, a reaction I was not long in hurling violently against her,

HÉLÈNE

blaming coldness on her part for having "cut my throat."
To regain my composure, to preserve my demeanor as a
man, I stared arrogantly at the whole of her body and my
eyes lingered deliberately on the parts which one cannot
stare at without indecency. I wanted to wound her mod-
esty, and I succeeded. Not a word was spoken.

VIII

Having returned home on Saturday, he was supposed to attend the great procession on Sunday; and it was at the procession that I saw him for the first time. The procession had an immense importance in the whole region; I too was on the square. I was waiting, moreover, to see *him*. Why had Hélène entreated me specially to come to the procession? I believed I knew what to think of the value of Hélène's religious feelings. A sun that was still very warm had reappeared over the countryside for the procession. One could therefore really say "It's parade weather." While the bells made a deafening racket with their three notes, I wandered confusedly about the square, slipping between the groups of peasants come from all corners of the valley, filled with anxiety over my fate. A strong-shouldered young girl wearing a black taffeta dress and walking at the head of the procession was carrying the brass crucifix backwards so that the body of Christ was turned towards the priests and the long motley snake of the procession: the three gazes of the three priests were fastened on the crucifix. In the

37

middle, wearing the cope, a weasel-faced priest from other parts; to his right, the village curé whom I recognized with horror by his glass eye. Next some Capuchin friars, numerous banners, and between two dark lines of the faithful who were telling their beads, the Madonna's palanquin, jumbled and sparkling, which six workers from the quarries were carrying on their shoulders, and the great gilded Virgin with the smooth look of a strange celestial doll setting her long earrings and her silver crown astir above her weary bearers. But I had still not got to the end of the emotion that great Virgin aroused in me when I saw them, him and her, behind. Directly after the procession came the lords of the country, surrounded by a margin of respect. Madame de Sannis, smiling, looked as though she were asleep as she walked; her eyes passed over me without seeing me. As for him—I of course had trouble seeing him; for a Capuchin, then Hélène, hid him from me. But people had not been exaggerating when they said to me that the man like a fortress was at first sight forbidding. The children's songs, then the choruses of men and women rose, incense smoked around the Virgin who, turned toward the four cardinal points and slightly inclined, gave her benediction to the crowd upon the square. Above the roofs gleamed the fresh snow of the Disgrazia. While the bells were rung their loudest, the Madonna reentered the church, after which the people came back out of it, and then I could look at the Count de Sannis, tall, a little stooped, who gave the impression of the most knotty sort of strength. His square-hewn face, his low forehead, his very slender nose between two deep wrinkles, and his jade-green eyes filled me with emotion, as did the whole sober military figure he represented; I was no less struck by the display of his Catholic faith, marked, furthermore, by a character of isolation. He did not speak to his wife, and yet the two Sannises were one.

A little later, Hélène introduced me, in the great Sannis salon with the dark furniture; it was very brief: he grasped my hand in his with cordiality (why had I given him my left hand?) and said to me that his sister-in-law's friend was welcome under his roof.

Afterwards, a door closed behind Count Humbert de Sannis, and I was not to see him again for a certain while, but I went into Hélène's small parlor, where I gazed at her for a long time in silence. She was . . . natural. Yet some look about her of feeling pleased disturbed me. Again I went close to her and forcefully buried my mouth in her Chevelure, I took plaits of her hair between my lips and then I kissed her secret skin. Hélène did not move her head, and a feeling almost like the feeling of the first kiss arose in both of us. Yet her face shone with joy and she said: "It's alright. Let's be calm."

From that day on in the Cas'alta there was the invisible colonel, Hélène most often in the small parlor with me, sometimes Hélène with him, and me by myself, and because of these diverse situations an uneasiness dug its chasm around my heart. I was now capable of knowing that I *loved* Hélène and I was becoming experienced enough to know that she also *loved me*. The remote but very real existence of Sannis in the house, despite the freedom left to Hélène, did not cease to have its effect: not even when he went away for a few days to hunt chamois in the mountain, for hunting was his only passion. I assumed his presence—wasn't that what Hélène once said to me? "You carry him inside you." But I could have answered Hélène that an imperceptible and essential thing had been continually fluctuating in her being since her husband's return. (I did not dare talk to her about her body as an organ; I was still far from knowing where man's love begins. Therefore I could not express in words to Hélène what my body unconsciously was telling me about her and what I dreaded hearing. I was beginning, during the ceremony of the kisses—and almost painfully—to divine in her the woman, the burning opposite sex, the sphinx.)

With liberality my mind admitted that there might be relations between her and her husband, and that they might do what they had always done (no doubt disfigured by the conjugal bond); to offset that, I opposed *my* kiss in the magic Chevelure. What I was pursuing was so much more mysterious and appeared to me so much more dangerous that I had nothing but scorn for the authorized relations of husband and wife. I called them the two H's and I thrust them far away from me; I kept Hélène. Hélène with her head of hair, Hélène trembling, Hélène panicked: thus I followed the steps that led to the woman she was with him, and I began to imagine her as such with me; and all her smiling, sublime nature, Hélène's dreamy power, I added them, with them I crowned the edifice: my Hélène.

But at the last moment an atrocious confusion arose in me at this thought; now I am going to say the thing (the essential and imperceptible thing that had fluctuated in

Hélène's being), the true thing that I had felt: that to be in her husband's bed again pleased Hélène. To be in it again calmed her, stilled her and lastly *changed* her, that is, changed her with relation to herself and changed her with relation to me, despite the overwhelming pressure of our affair of kisses. Sleeping with Sannis "did her good," to put it bluntly, and it was this "good" that suddenly devastated my heart, that devastated it in unsuspected places. It was not, I have shown, simple jealousy, since Hélène had divided herself into two parts. A more extraordinary devastation. "Imagine what the pure and glacial waters of the lake at Sils may feel when they receive the mud-laden mountain stream, though it is their source"—it was thus that I tried to make my anguish reasonable, in a phrase written to Hélène.

(From this point onward I wrote to Hélène; she sometimes answered me, little notes folded in four that we delivered to one another.)

I am still trying to understand the nature of that devastation. It was also as though my strength had been slashed. I can say nothing more *true*: in this there is the idea of a substance that grows with joy, with abundance, with hope, that receives a blow, that falls cut halfway through. To receive the death-blow. Is it death? Was I born in order to die? Or was I born dead? . . . And so on. When I indulged in these frightful thoughts in regard to Hélène (not allowing her to see a single one of these morbid thoughts) sweat would cover my forehead, and I would feel I was falling into a *hole* where I was going to spin until I lost consciousness. I clung to everything, to her, to the furniture, to things . . . to every outward thing.

My malaise would no sooner subside than I would distinctly see in my memory, in fullest detail, the marriage of the woman in black which I had witnessed in a dream, and the Woman in Black who was surely the unfortunately wed Hélène.

IX

Another source of conflict lay in the admiration I felt for this man Sannis.

Little by little I began to admire him. I almost never caught sight of him, yet I perceived him within a frame that favored his balanced movements; I felt he was strong, and upright, honest to the bone.

In order to leave me in his wife's company, as he did (with a manner that, far from humiliating me, elevated my situation), he had either to be the soul of confidence or wise from much experience of love; for he loved her. I thought a great deal about this man out of the Middle Ages. To think about him was more compelling than my aversion or my principles. Did he have to have in his hands what I loved? I would have adored him. For he represented to me everything that I wanted to be. Hard, but also mild; always in the simplicity of himself. Energetic, he made no noise with his energy. About him admirable stories were told (I got people to talk) of constancy and cool-headedness. A life to save on the mountain, a catastrophe to avert for the countryside, and the Count de Sannis was the first to set off and the first on the spot. A remarkable soldier, his men worshipped him, he had gone to war as a corporal in the infantry, but refusing all decorations. Too much the soul of honor to place his honor in an object. His acts became him. He almost never spoke. He was a believing Catholic in the Catholic Church. I no longer saw any divergence, when I looked at him, among all these authentic virtues. His wife was his possession, and he said "vous" to her, but he left her free or rather responsible. In the same way, he knew how to hold her. I admired his knowing how to hold her, I admired his holding her, but all of a sudden I hated him for that! He was truly a tower of a man on whom his wife must lean, whether she would or no, in order to resist other men. His was truly the strength and natural resilience of the country embodied in a man of its breed. Obviously his experiences were simple, even crude, but his way of experiencing expressed the most refined civilization. Even his Holbein figure I found admirable.

But what put me most at his feet was the feeling I had for him as a hunter. Here something like a shadow formed in my love for Hélène, for she scorned hunting. But when at day's end I saw the Count de Sannis pressing his weary step upon the round cobbles of the village lanes, his rifle pointed downward, while behind him a man spotted with fresh blood bore the ibex with its bound feet and dreamy dead eye, then my own blood seemed to stop in my veins, and I would almost have wanted to be the dead ibex in order to have had the glory of being hunted by him! I felt every detail in that scene, the gentle beast's unjustified agony, the Count's severe law, felt everything with such violence that I did not know how to vent that violence in the two directions of hatred and of admiration, and remained the better part of an hour motionless in a lane or a corridor. Just imagine how complicated my condition was if, a short time before, I had had my anguished pleasure with Hélène.

I could not even look calmly upon his weapons, his more or less blood-stained clothing, and his bag, displayed on a chest in the entrance as he had taken them off. Hatred and affection would instantly revive in a whirlwind of dust overspreading a devastated terrain. I would have liked to go with him. I would have liked to leave behind me the superb Hélène and put her out of my thoughts. I would have liked to lose the smell of Hélène and the Chevelure and gain this other smell.

Yet I turned back toward Hélène. Hélène was magnetic; her seduction did not have an entirely human character. It was as though she were reading the real situation the way one reads a letter written in invisible ink, by exposing it to flame. Why didn't she talk to me more? Why did she allow love to suffer in every way possible? She did not even say to me: I love you. I did not say it to her either, even though our lips were swollen with it. Was she waiting for me to be the one, was I waiting for her to be the one? However it may have been, and probably in order to punish ourselves, we soon decided to give up those exhausting kisses in the Chevelure: this was also in the hope of a more important scene that had to take place and that we did not yet want to foresee.

Alone, I thought more and more about her body, about her sex. I imagined what it must be like, but no—I did

not at first dare picture it to myself. A shadow? A jasmine
flower? A human Venus's-shell? Was it dark, or light? I
trembled to my very soul. It was thus that the idea came
to me of taking a dried rose leaf and a living pansy flower,
of applying them to my sex, and then of sending them to
her in a closed envelope with a note that told her what I
had done and asking her to do the same thing. The next
day I received her gift, just like mine! I experienced a
fresh access of terrible, insane joy. I frenetically kissed
"her" flowers. Their scent was tender, strange, melancholy. When we were in each other's presence again, we
did not speak of our exchange. As though *another life*
were beginning gently, cautiously. In this way it allowed
me to dream of Hélène as a sexual being and to cast upon
Hélène the gaze that corresponded. I was impatiently
awaiting the end of an affectionate afternoon, in order,
once back in my own privacy, to send her something new,
and I barely answered the remarks she made to me because I was seeking how to advance farther and to divine
her even more fully on a flower.

It was then, at the afternoon's end, that Hélène de
Sannis who appeared to be suffering from fear, fear mingled with ardor and with growing ardor, all of a sudden
turned to me under her head of hair and with the sim-
plest expression in the world said to me: I love you. And
when she made that blinding avowal to me, I sensed all
her strength as erotic foster-mother of men. I closed my
eyes instinctively; and then there appeared a vision that I
have always preserved in my mind: that of the Stranger.
The Stranger—it wasn't she and it wasn't I, but different
from her, from me, and from us; it was perhaps: us. The

Stranger was covered over everywhere with a brilliant sheen of Pleasure as with a varnish; the sensuous pleasure alien to love (better, war) was his function. At the same time he was atrocious and wanted only to "see." I'm not sure how to describe this Stranger nor how to say what he signified; I am not sure the Stranger was anything other than the Chevelure—the Helmet of Gold—or than her naked under the Chevelure.

I went off beaming, swaggering, and torn apart. In a state of exaltation because of the certainty of being loved—but *had she really said* I love you?—I was all the more impatient to send her another exciting, perverse message—pursuing along two different lines my diabolical love—but fearing "the stranger" who was forcing us to take action. The time of our trials was beginning and danger was speeding toward us upon its evil wings.

X

I was in the large dark salon, busily smoking a cigarette to relieve my agitation. The weather was fine, as usual, and when it was fine the house was dark. I thought of her in order to think about myself. I believed I was alone and tranquil. I descended into her all the way down to her living mystery and the place of that mystery. I was horrified and happy and stopped there. Suddenly I heard sounds of her. One of the windows had been left wide open, I was inside, she was outside. She was walking with her husband and talking at the same time. They both knew, however, that I was there in the parlor. They were chatting. They were walking on the flagged pathway in the garden. I did not know what they were saying; I wasn't paying attention to that anyway, because I was waiting for Sannis to finish and Hélène to come join me. All of this was absurd. Led nowhere. But an invincible force brought me back to thinking of her as secret flesh, wondrous, dionysiac. While I daydreamed in this odd way they continued to talk and their conversation truly went on and on. My torture made me listen, but I had to

reject at once what I heard, because nothing clear remained in my mind. —Why was it lasting for so long? I
lit a second, then a third cigarette. I could have gone out
and shown myself. But I preferred to remain on my guard,
at the far end of the vast room. I could wait as long as
they liked. They understood this, because they entered
the salon just after having spoken a name, a name that he
uttered, that she repeated, and that was thus engraved on
my mind: *Pauliet.*

Immediately I remembered having involuntarily read
"Pauliet" on the outside of an envelope, in her room.
And right away there followed from it another memory:
that of having entered her room without announcing myself (thinking she was in another part of the house) and
having seen her on her knees putting some letters away in
her special little cupboard, a bundle of blue letters over
which she was weeping.

I think it was at that moment that the Count de Sannis
told me of the arrival of his nephew Pauliet, "a compan-
ion just about your age," and that I frowned, and that
Hélène looked at me so attentively. Then Hélène looked
at her husband and then she ceased looking at anything.

As soon as I was alone with Hélène I asked her who he
was, Poyet, or Pauliet. (I hadn't yet got clear hold of the
name.) "Who is Pauliet?"—I asked it with a certain
sharpness, for it seemed to me (oddly) that the two Sannises were sporting with me, and that right away—what-
ever Pauliet might be—I had to recapture my Hélène.
"And you spoke of him tenderly, once, as you were clos-
ing your cupboard." Hélène appeared to be very moved.
She gave me the following explanation. Pauliet was a

nephew of Monsieur de Sannis. Motherless from the time
of his birth, Pauliet, even though he was by nature a
person of quality, had been the cause of torment to the
whole family and particularly to her, Hélène. But he remained dear to all, perhaps in spite of his faults . . .
Pauliet was ill, that was the long and short of it. "Monsieur de Sannis asked him to come, without consulting
me beforehand. If my opinion had been asked I would
probably have objected that this was not the most favorable time. I'm afraid you won't like him . . ." she added
softly, pale, addressing me with the intimate "tu." The
caress of that "tu" made my suspicion give ground, but as
soon as I heard that a room was being readied for Pauliet,
my suspicion came rushing back. "Not the most favorable time"—what did she mean by that? Was I, then, on
the same footing as this Pauliet, in other words was he on
the same footing as I? Or *had he been* on the footing
where I now was? Ever since the arrival of Colonel de
Sannis, *she had known* that her husband had invited the
wayward boy. And there had been such *intimacy* between
Hélène and me since that arrival! And yet she had said
nothing to me about the threat that was hanging over our
amorous solitude; on the contrary, she had told me her
husband would soon be leaving for the army again. And
this Pauliet who was to come here to rest his nerves, how
long would he stay? etc., etc. My imagination was working in the direction of mistrust. Little details aided it.
Hélène had several portraits of men in her room; one of
them, particularly well placed, was of Pauliet. They were
preparing for the coming of Pauliet as for that of a reg-
ular visitor: in fact, the chambermaid told me that he had

not been up for nearly two years, but that, before, Monsieur Pauliet was there all the time; and right away I saw in the eyes, around the mouth, and on the skin of this lively girl a certain glow of pleasure . . . The mention of Pauliet's name produced a curious shared response, whether between Hélène and her husband, or between her and the servants. She kept letters from Pauliet locked up in her famous cupboard. Lastly—and this seemed to me the sign indicative of former amours—she never spoke of him first or of her own accord; she answered, when the subject of him arose; and she cared about everything that concerned him.

When I had contemplated Hélène as an adulterous woman, I had imagined she could be so in a general way, and with me; never would I have supposed she might have been that with others! I saw her as adulterous, figuratively. Whereas now (to follow the bent of my instinctive speculation) I saw her, I had the direct intuition of her, in the flesh: which hurt.

Then one morning Pauliet was there, and I shook his hand after being introduced. He was not at all what I was expecting.

A handsome boy, pale, in appearance accommodating, with the skin of a woman. Pretty hair naturally curly, quivering nostrils, he had the beauty of the south. My two first impressions were: he seems good, and human—and he is very ill.

Pauliet was coughing. He was coughing with the elegance of an artist. Pauliet would smile as he coughed. His smile was a smile so intense and so full of an atrocious or sublime experience, that during the first moment I looked only at his smile, I studied his smile. How was he able to smile like that? Then I turned my eyes toward Hélène, without warning, to see if she would not betray some old feelings, a particular attachment to this smile of revolution and seduction; Hélène's face was cool, oval, and smooth for Pauliet, her face was burning and smooth for me, for her husband her face showed concern.

The very next day, seeking Pauliet's company, I took a walk with him. We went into the broad meadow where I had encountered Hélène for the first time. He was still very tired from the trip; and this was no doubt why he did not find the meadow as beautiful as I myself had found it, and besides, a certain change had come about, for it was autumn now, and the peasants were strewing a bad-smelling manure over the grass; at least this was the way I formulated the thing at first. But Pauliet said to me: "I don't like mountains. Mountains look as though they are preaching to you. I care only for cities and love." He had seen a lot: Paris, Vienna, and Rome, "cities where there are women," were familiar places to him. He spoke several languages, which was helpful, "even though in every city you speak *the* language, the same one everywhere." By noon, walking with him, I was drunk from the alcohol that rose from his conversation, from his subtle, quick, elegant remarks—interrupted by rather long fits of coughing. The remarks bore on women's bodies, their prettiest points, their preferred places, pleasures with them, what they liked best, what they liked least, according to the country and the species, what one had to do to them to get them to be accommodating, and how to play with them. He called things by their names, with a crudity, but also a grace, that were both irresistible. All sorts of women, nude or costumed, in complicated postures with men in couples, in trios, in chains, passed before my eyes just as simply as you please and remained in my mind like a demoniac "engraving." I knew all that, I had even come into contact with it, and yet everything was new. Remarks full of daring in which appeared ways of living, of behaving, portraits, views from below, aspects of streets, rooms, alcoves—which were far, far, and incredibly far from here! Yet it seemed to me that Hélène was listening to our licentious conversation and liked something about it, and this idea caused me pleasure as though Hélène de Sannis *were part of* the female material of which we were so fond, *both of us*. One day soon after, Pauliet told me that, disgusted with bourgeois family life, he had gone to live among girls, he meant whorehouse girls, in houses where the working class clientele didn't "fool about," for he scorned the false elegance of the high-class brothels; and that "nowhere had he been so at his ease for thinking about eternal things." "All honor to women and to marriage with them! Marriage is the exquisite natural state such as we can still experience it after having been irremediably disabled by civilization. A girl in heat who has only her organ and her elastic shape is as beautiful as the Parthenon. I am an ancient Greek, my dear; like the Greeks, I love all forms and all sexes." I looked at him even more attentively at these words. His cheekbones pink as though rouged, his mouth wet and fleshy, two ashen circles under his eyes, he appeared to be a man aflame with a devouring idea, as brilliant as a star in the sky. He displayed by turns a virile

aggressivity and the submissiveness of a woman. Under-
lying his licentiousness was a frenetic love, a love of love,
anonymous, all the more love because no figure of any
sex received it; if he was perverse, as he liked to say, and
if he liked a low form of copulation, it could only be in
order to augment his thirst, and out of *fear* "that his thirst
could be quenched." When we returned from our first
walk he said to me:

"These days (when I'm not in the venerable Sannis
house) I screw a woman every afternoon at five o'clock.
That's how I fight the disease" (he began coughing).

"But don't you see how the disease is aggravated by
everything you do? Your illness is in your chest, isn't it?"

"In my chest, yes, my dear. As long as I have a frazzle
of it left here"—he pointed to his belly—"I'll put it to
use! Nothing to be done about it."

We arrived at Hélène's house.

XI

The effect of Pauliet's presence was to revive the obsessive idea I had had of Hélène; as though I were choosing the wrong path. From those faraway times I have preserved a fetish piece of paper that I had sewn into a pocket of my jacket, that I afterward kept as a sign of my madness. It was a face powder paper that she had smoothed over her skin during a walk; on it I had inscribed in a column all the names I knew for a woman's parts.

Whereas these horrible tendencies—and also love, indifferent to them—had appeared to retreat before the potent presence of Monsieur de Sannis and my odd attachment to him, now everything began again even more intensely. The main argument was to claim that by these means I already had her, without having to arrive at the reality of taking her. Didn't she write to me at the close of one of her notes: "She whom you will have, she whom you so much have already." But what I did not see was that by allowing me to believe that "I already had her so much," these monstrous images that gathered before my mind's eye were going to prevent me from having her. I resumed sending my intimate, symbolic communications. She always answered with a message of equivalent signification, chosen with grace, and the finds we hit upon overwhelmed me with perverse joy. I soon imagined that the love we were making was more extraordinary than all known kinds of love, and Pauliet's stories seemed to me interesting to the extent that they helped me by expediting for me the invention of forms of eroticism that Pauliet could not suspect. Beyond that, certain relations had been established between Pauliet and me on the subject of Hélène, in the following manner.

Pauliet was clever and with his air of not seeming to pry he knew the art of asking questions. He found out very quickly that I had neither mistress nor sister nor girlfriends, but that in my life at the moment there was "a woman"; in addition he had his own idea of Hélène, an idea whose exact value I was unable to arrive at; and he had his eye on us all the time. I was with him in the meadow again, at the spot where I had met Hélène, when he asked me point-blank what I thought of the particular charm, variously appreciated, of his aunt—whom he called "my cousin." I answered coolly that that charm was in fact profound and mysterious. "Mysterious!" cried Pauliet with a burst of laughter. "Mysterious!" And he said nothing more about it, still amused. I felt that I was receiving a wound and that I could not "let it go," but immediately afterwards I saw that I had been found out. He was looking at me in a fondling and mocking way. My anger confused me. I was caught in his net. What was I to do? Slap him? But one doesn't protect the mystery of love by striking arguments. He saw me blush to the roots of my hair. He put his arm through mine. "Come, my dear fellow, confess that you love her." "Yes, of course, I love her," I said defenselessly. "That's lovely, lovely, very lovely." He whistled softly to himself. This time I wondered whether I wasn't going to kill him. "However, I'm going to say something impertinent to you. But you won't get angry, will you, my dear fellow?" Unsettled by the confession I had made, I shook my head no. "I've noticed the shape of your nose. Well, it's the sort that can sniff out lewdness . . . As for her, she's a wet-nurse to young men. You will succeed, it will be magnificent—oh, I promise you!—'a fine marriage'." I wondered what was going to happen between us. But I was already pulling myself back together, I was playing the game. "You're quite mistaken," I said to him. "If I have somewhat ardent feelings for your cousin, she doesn't know it, thank the Lord. So let us leave it like that." "And your sister?" he answered me, bantering. "If you don't hide your little business from me, I, Pauliet, will be able to help you."

The secret had been uncovered, by him, and in what manner! I resigned myself to it. No, I didn't; there remained, to beguile my mind, the atrocious idea: "Has he had the Chevelure, did he possess the Chevelure before me?" It will be magnificent . . . The wet-nurse to young men . . . I will be able to help you . . .

I decided that he could not have had the Chevelure—not at least such as it had shaped itself in my mind; how could this dissolute fellow have had the Chevelure, since it was I who had conceived of the symbol, and since the Chevelure, Hélène's mystery, was *I*? And yet I longed to

know what he had done, what he had had, for he had had
something from Hélène; whether she had felt passion for
him, or whether he had seduced her. I wanted to "see"
them together in order to rid myself of that odious past.
But Pauliet, too, was keeping his lips sealed; and when
his lips were sealed they were perfectly sealed, as is always the case with men who live in intrigues with women.
I divined nothing.

It was much too late to detect anything at all that
would have shown me that Hélène had bestowed her
favors on him.

Yes, he did say something to me. And this detail had its
importance. He asked me: "How old would you say she
was?" I refrained from venturing an opinion. I felt that
this time he would bring out what he intended to say.
"Look, you find her so beautiful. Thirty-three, thirty-six?
You figure she's under forty." It was true, in the eyes of
my heart it was impossible that Hélène could be forty.
"Once you become very *close* to her, she will perhaps tell
you she is thirty-five. Well, my dear, she's forty-three.
Forty-three years old," he repeated, separating the sylla-
bles. "And you, how old are you?" I barked at him, and
I gave the ill boy an unkind look; he was startled. "I? I'll
be twenty-three next cherry harvest." And he shrugged
his shoulders without being able to carry the joke any
farther.

As for me, I was deep in meditation on "age" and ages,
and on insoluble and inexorable questions ressembling
enigmas. Born before me, born after her, after him, what
was the meaning of these somber decrees of fate? Why
she and why I, thus placed and patterned? But I felt the

power of the decrees and I evaluated all the real things that were consequent upon this first violence of nature. Weren't the two births always there, perceptible? Did I love her because she was born so long before me? Did she have to love men born many years after her? Many years after her—wasn't that like the child she hadn't had? Oh, could I go farther into her soul and into her body, into Hélène's destiny? I repeated the numbers to myself: forty-three—and seventeen.

XII

A smile is a thing that can appear insane. In this strange
act there is rending, revelation, fire. She smiles at me. She
opens her mouth halfway, she uncovers a little of the
mucous interior, lips and gums, all wet; most especially
she shows her teeth, her shining teeth, always white, of
ivory, her teeth also wet; at the same moment she has
distended her flesh and she opens the orifice in it. What
an orifice! Burning red—every other orifice is present in
this one. It is the orifice of love, that of thought. Then a
light appears that seems to rise from her mouth, unless
perchance it falls into it. It is also the orifice for eating,
devouring, retaining food. It is impossible to say what the
magic of light consists of, whether it is the light of her
lips, or the light of her teeth, or the light of her breath,
but all of this, in light, avows: "I am here, it is I, I am, for
you." One wouldn't have thought one could see her right
away so nude in broad daylight. One wouldn't have
thought this cannibalism possible. The simultaneous pro-
posal and acceptance can be read in these tall teeth gleam-
ing with saliva and yet menacing, can be read in these

eyes full of sparks and tears, and in this illuminating flesh which from eye to lip bring the smile together. And in the shadow of the perfect light there is something resembling crime.

I had never seen a smile . . . I was seeing a smile for the first time. I was opening in her face the door that gave on her inner being.

Hélène smiled at me with that smile *unwitting of itself,* for several minutes on end, in the small boxwood garden. She looked at me, she smiled at me, she imposed silence on me. She forced me to remain motionless and watch her smile.

Why was it necessary to run to Pauliet afterwards?

Where lay the need I felt for him? For I regarded him as an enemy, capable of diminishing me. I felt neither trust nor affection. —Or rather, yes, I felt some affection. Fearing his advice, I hoped to receive it. I envied him with disgust and I was jealous of his capacity for cynicism. I was fascinated by him. (In sum, I had somewhat the same feelings toward him that I had had for the Count de Sannis at first; but in a more ignoble register.) My aversion, finally, outweighed my sympathy: then why go and show him the reflection, however dimmed it might be, of the prime happiness of my life?

In truth I believed my behavior was very rational in character (and I believed too that I regarded myself with no very high esteem for proceeding on this plane), and already I was calling myself a *demon.* I now knew that in me there existed a demon, that it was this demon that had to turn Hélène into an experience, and that between this demon, which conveyed Hélène's sex everywhere, and another demon, Pauliet's demon, communications were destined to be established, an alliance was going to be concluded. At what moment did we reach the secret agreement? Whether that day or the next, it hardly matters. The two demons were going to help each other, probably in opposition to the woman, it appeared. I had wanted to take another road, a road of my own, against Pauliet; I still wanted this; but an event like the smile that I had just received immediately had very serious consequences, by engendering *disarray*. Disarray is a sort of *suffering* and it was under pressure from suffering that my demon rushed toward its brother. Was suffering going to prevent me from playing my game or any game at all? This was why I was led to think in a vague but very powerful way that being so close to the goal I must now "get there." I had a program of action and I did not know what it was. Pauliet was going to "teach me something." Such really was my thought. Yet I did not want to tell him anything, show him anything.

. . . My obsession with the multiple images of forms, the imagined bestial odor of musk and secret humors, the play of eyes that sketch, so to speak, the bear's shag and flesh mingled, with the details of placement and aspect, and the *life* that this has, this continual imagining, warm, eager, by now sharp to the point of pain and agreeable to the point of provoking tears—I was quite incapable of ridding myself of it; but with Pauliet I kept repressing it so that he could not possibly see anything of it; what I asked of Pauliet, what I wanted to draw from him, I would then adopt it for use within my world formed of these images, I would espouse it—in order (if possible) to *get there*.

However, Pauliet said more or less this to me: every love contains an abyss that is Pleasure; pleasure is all that is real; therefore leap into the abyss, into pleasure. Leap, therefore, leap into the abyss. There is only this abyss of what is "true" in love. The charms to which you are abandoning yourself (you think you're hiding it from me) are pleasant elements, certainly, but without the plunge into the abyss all this fades even as it occurs. Leap, so that this may be real, only leap into the abyss.

Into the abyss . . .

I did not know why his "abyss" had for me a meaning altogether other than that which he gave to it; this meaning was primarily that of *death*. Pauliet, without knowing it, or knowing it, was making a certain use of death. The death with which he had some contacts, perhaps, with which he was carrying on a flirtation. Often we went walking in the cemetery, for the particularly fine view one had there; the poetry of that little terrace pleased him very much: he walked with pleasure over the invisible graves. Perhaps, in the end, all of Pauliet's debauchery was an experience of Death. Nor did Hélène seem to me unimpaired by that spirit, safe from the abyss, from death, from pleasure mingled with death. Did this attract me? Or repel me? No—I loathed death, I loathed it! But it was impossible for me not to make an exception for Hélène's sensibility, and in favor of the little cemetery.

. . . During the weeks that I spent with Pauliet my judgment changed a great deal and I became attached to him. I gradually perceived the beauty, the discreet quality of his being, the libertine's cloak once put aside. I even sensed his despair, his unhappiness, carefully hidden from the others. I was so aware of his merit that I lost all interest in the Count de Sannis, even though my relations with him were good. Hélène, and Pauliet, occupied the whole of my vision.

XIII

With the end of the autumn Pauliet felt less well. I saw
him in his bedroom several times. He was subject to
sudden rises of temperature toward the evening; this temperature turned into fever. Hélène, in the sort of sus-
pense in which we all existed, at once seemed worried. It
was with a charming pout of his lip that Pauliet would
announce: "Thirty-eight point four this evening," but
under his laughter I read distress, the abrupt distress of
an ill person whose illness is reputed to be insidious. His
good humor—"Resting won't have had a favorable effect
upon me"—scarcely lasted more than four days, and with
an extreme, a furious nervousness, Pauliet put together
plans, took them apart, announced at last that he would
be leaving for the valley, because, he said, Sogno's cli-
mate did not agree with him, too many barometric
changes, too much wind, "and because there was too
much agitation in this house," the latter argument having
inevitably to be interpreted as a piece of gratuitous spite
toward Hélène. The Sannises discussed the matter and it
was decided that Pauliet would go spend some time in

the Château de Ponte, down below, where all the necessary arrangements would be made. Pauliet left that same day. Despite my efforts, I could not find out what Hélène was thinking.

I was astonished to see how far Monsieur de Sannis' goodness extended toward his nephew. Before the latter's departure in the carriage, the Count himself covered Pauliet's shoulders and legs with a large Scotch plaid. Sannis put aside his concerns with his property and hunting in order to keep Pauliet company in what I imagined to be "the boring Château de Ponte." —On the other hand, I was delighted to sense a profound indifference and a disdain in Hélène. Once her initial emotion had subsided, she watched him leave quite coldly. I said goodbye to Pauliet; and the carriage disappeared. Hélène shrugged her shoulders. Nevertheless, I thought she was sad.

There was an enormous upwelling of love. Days passed that resembled, through their characteristic of warm illusion, those I had known four months earlier, just after Torre. But Hélène telephoned Ponte often. The ailing boy's condition was the same. Pauliet seemed cheerful, and "It is extraordinary," Hélène said, "how the presence of my husband helps him and magnetizes him. The same thing happened two years ago." But Hélène murmured: "Pauliet incarnates the sin of Monsieur de Sannis."

Two days later, Hélène announced to me: "I have to go down. Pauliet is worse. This time I'm worried." She entreated me, suddenly vehement, to stay there and wait for her. "I beg you, my little lion, I, Hélène, beg you!"

66

She said several times "my little lion," words I had not heard before and which submerged me in burning joy.

I had no further news during the next few days. No doubt the illness was worsening. My situation was difficult, for distress was coming at me from all sides. I did not dare telephone Ponte, once again gripped by my former timidities. At the same time, and as though expressly, my family was taking me very harshly to task in endless letters and threatening to cut off my funds. Hélène did not write. The days were treacherous and the winter season's sun, shining too splendidly in a crystalline atmosphere, made the heart ache. It was hard for me to think of Hélène in any manner. I now lived on nothing but the hope of seeing her come back soon.

I was in the privacy of my room in the middle of the night. The moon in its third quarter still shed a very peculiar light, and near it the stars, because of the frosty night, sparkled furiously and seemed abnormally large. Ever since the sun had gone down a feeling that I could not formulate had been seeking an outlet. By the light of the contemplative moon I understood what I wanted to do. I understood what I had to do. Hélène de Sannis was standing before me, for the first time in a long time, entirely alive, and she was looking at me with curiosity, saying to me "my little lion." I uncovered myself. I was not surprised to see that I was entirely ready for her. Oh, today it was for her! The first stirrings of my pleasure were vague and profound, as though coming from very far away, and I felt that there would be a long wait. I cannot say how long this went on before the moment when, separating from the depths, the current began to rise. This wave, this current, this rise for Hélène occurred with an incredible slowness, but with a force to which I was totally attentive. When it decided to come forth, the liquid almost brought me pain through the slow contraction that augmented my pleasure to the point of delirium: it was coming, it was coming out, and it came out! Hélène! I saw a bouquet of living anemones. I also saw a scythe which, once the flowers had blossomed in that unconsummated joy, lopped them and left them severed on the ground.

. . . I returned to myself, having performed my first act as a man for Hélène, for that was how I interpreted what had happened. And she had to know it. With mysterious precautions I collected a little of the liquid in a glass.

The next day my feelings were different. A touch of hatred mingled with the still brilliant color. Unsure what she was going to say, I was full of aversion. I nevertheless had "the courage" to pour the liquor into a little flask and to send the flask to Ponte by mail. Ten times I was on the point of taking the package back. Package in hand, I would approach the post office and then turn away. At last I sent it off, *out of faithfulness.* —No! I did not doubt Hélène. She would know the meaning of all things. But aversion in the extreme—I think it was that—seized me at the particular moment of the act, in as much as it concluded a whole series of childish and perverse acts, to introduce us, with Hélène, into the terrible act, finally promised.

From Hélène—at Pauliet's side—there came no sign to make me believe she had received something, no response.

She telephoned me; from her voice I clearly sensed that I had "touched" her, but this feeling was riddled by others, for example by the feeling of the sadness in her voice. She was telephoning me about Pauliet, who was in the grip of the fever. And I didn't understand what was happening! We are so locked up inside our own stories.

Hélène's conversations on the telephone were laconic, with a very tender nuance to them. When she talked to me that day I was about to tell her I was preparing to go down to Ponte in order to see her, even if only for an hour; but in a toneless voice she said things that seemed to me unconnected and only increased my anguish. She stopped speaking. I understood that she was preparing me for some news. She said:

"Pauliet is dead."

Dead! My heart turned over. The sound of Hélène's voice faded. "Hello!" she cried, "are you there?" Hélène was talking into the phone; Pauliet's end had been sudden, rapid, and without pain. I heard this from very very far away through a sickening buzz in my ears. "Pauliet died in a Christian manner."

Dead, oh my God. Dead.

A very quick letter from Hélène received that evening told me: "After this dreadful misfortune it would be preferable that you not come down. Yet I ask you to wait. —Be, still and always, the little lion whom I love. —I will be at Sogno Monday"—it was then Friday—"for by then he will have been taken away to be buried in the family cemetery. Your H."

XIV

But she changed her mind. She telegraphed to me:
"Come down to Ponte. Arrive Monday."

It is difficult to describe in just what state of mind I left
Sogno. The countryside was shrouded in mists. It no
longer looked familiar. Yet the tragic fervor that was still
increasing inside me, the impression of living out a drama,
the certainty I had that I was now going toward my destiny, left horrible suffering, terror, grief almost unable to
get through to me. I aged in those few days. My inmost
thought was divided between shame and hope. —The
ride in the cart lasted one hour and I was at Ponte.

Sad twilight. Ponte was a straggling village. The mountain heights, seen from here, were wilder, more enormous
and the wall they formed more dismal because one could
barely make out (through the shreds of mist) anything
beyond some of the lower parts of the rocks which at
Sogno formed a silvery line against the sky. The forests
fell upon the village like night. There were no sounds of
life when, at the last turn, I had the cart stop.

I saw the village of Ponte, houses of wood and light-colored stucco, closely huddled, poor-looking. In front, like a block of white stone, the château. We went on further down.

Everything seemed mournful to me, of a sadness that contained fire, but fire with no outlet. Of the château's exterior nothing caught my notice but the very high white carriage gateway with its large arch and its small pediment forming a roof, and in the middle the Sannises' shield, the same coat of arms I had so often contemplated on the rustic ceiling of Hélène's parlor, but here in granite.

Pauliet's coffin had passed through this gateway and traveled between the meadows down there, between their little board fences.

And to the right of the majestic gateway, in the twilight, the lofty house. And I also recall, as making upon me a unique impression at my arrival, the misty willows on one side and on the other the twenty great sandstone curbs guarding the facade. Then, to my eyes, everything in that first evening became a whirling confusion. I was welcomed; nevertheless everything was dominated by a horrible silence. I remember blinding chandeliers and long vistas. Amidst all that my mind must quickly have begun to wander. But—I saw her. She was in black, as beautiful as an enchantress.

What we first said must have been insignificant—or else singularly grave and full of importance—for it has vanished from my memory. The gaiety of the lights appalled me. She had most of the lamps put out and a relative darkness isolated us together. I saw then that she was alone at Ponte. For we were eating at a table where

there were only two seats. Little by little I discovered my
surroundings. It was a very noble room, the one in which
we were dining, entirely panelled in natural wood panelling like her parlor up the mountain. I ventured quick
glances in Hélène's direction, seeking her within this au-
thentically Sannis décor. But her features slipped away
toward the night and the night's things. I noticed that the
beauty of her flesh which I saw as true (as though it
wasn't her at all) had intensified and become more material. Yes, Hélène was more material. After the meal, she
stood before me, in black, and gestured to me to follow
her. We had not said a single word about Pauliet. I followed her down a hallway underneath high white vaults.
At its end were two short, straight stairways and a bare
little door. That door, which I saw as "bare," had a
singular effect on me, as though it were attracting me to
it; I sensed the moment of knowing a thing that I did not
want to know. The door, narrow in the solid stone wall,
had a sort of monastic aspect and seemed in some sense
not in keeping with the earlier rooms that I had confusedly passed through in the château. But wasn't I walking behind Hélène as I went through the door? A small
gallery, suspended above the garden, brought us, her and
me, to the threshold of a low-ceilinged room, a very cosy
reading room with an adjoining bedroom—the annex, as
I was to learn later, rebuilt expressly for Pauliet by Monsieur de Sannis and more recent than the rest of the
château. "It was here," Hélène said to me in a dull and
expressionless voice. She showed me the couch in the
bedroom. "He died here, the poor thing," she continued.
"At ten in the morning there was a first spitting of blood.

His fever rose very high. Ice-packs did nothing and at four o'clock he spat blood again, much more. After which he was given the sacraments; at six o'clock he died. We were with him. His death seemed completely mechanical. There wasn't the least bit of love in his death," Hélène said in a thoughtful voice. She mused for a moment. "I don't think he suffered at all." I was surprised and at the same time satisfied by the dryness of Hélène's tone. It freed me of my anguish. In the presence of this extraordinary woman, death, love, no longer had the meaning they generally have.

I asked her where Monsieur de Sannis was. "He left," she said simply, "to accompany Pauliet's body. He will not come back here for several months, because he is going to reassume a command. We are alone!" she said with a tragic vivacity, and at that moment I felt that, finally, I hated the Count de Sannis. Did I hate him because of her and because he was treating her so badly, or because I was obliged to revise my own opinion of him and suffer because of him, or because of the love between Hélène and me? Had he nothing to do with Pauliet's death? If someone had prevented me from being at Pauliet's deathbed, it was he. I hated him. She had trembled when she uttered his name—whereas when she told me about Pauliet's end she was as calm as a statue. Thus this man was terrorizing her in some way, which in all our time at Sogno I had never noticed. That he left his wife a clear field was no proof of his nobility! For I grasped the indirect form of his action and of his war, pursued within Hélène by means of the sense of death that Hélène had to such a degree. (One speaks so *coldly* only about what

horrifies one.) I felt detached from him, rid of my culpability in his regard. And I ardently longed that Hélène
might regain, in my arms, her as yet lost strength as
nurturer.

Hélène wept. I wept too, without daring to touch her.

XV

The next day . . .

The next day everything was luminous and pink, the sun shone brightly. It was not only the Château de Ponte that appeared enchanted in the freshness among the lofty vaporous mountains. Enchanted also were the communications that had taken place during the night between the beings that sleep, a decree of destiny that had been pronounced, so that a fragrance of life almost overpowering in its savor and color entered through the window, coming from a magnificent shabby garden, and that all the things I saw as I strayed from room to room in the château, in addition to their own beauty, contained the same revelation.

I did not see Hélène anywhere.

It was then that I discovered those white and colored stuccos of such perfect tenderness of taste, the ceilings, light but heavy with volutes and sculpted motifs which in each room seemed each to be lost in its own ecstasy, those lofty convent corridors, those doors framed in marble, those immense varied rooms—in short, that Baroque

palpitating and cruel; the entrance in green and pink of a
pastry material with the old rusted arms; and at the foot
of the angular, military stairway, swung down over the
entrance, the red curtain. A red theater curtain, strangled
in the middle by an enormous cord, a blood-colored
hanging out of Shakespeare, had a disturbing effect there:
one couldn't be sure it wasn't a trompe-l'oeil. This is a
pell-mell recounting of what I chanced upon—in surprise, and in the happiness that came to me from the
night—at the outset of my wanderings, and if I speak
right away about the red hanging it is because having
seen it by chance as I turned around, I was so struck that
I had to go touch it. The marvellous was here in harmony
with the superb, the sensual with the spare—leading also
to craziness. All this had a name: it was Hélène. I walked
on, as I came upon other beauties I murmured: Hélène.
Hélène was in front of me. She said hello to me. She was
not in black. Her eyes were paler than usual. We had
enountered one another off the entry in the great room
flagged in alpine stone, of a particular spareness, ante-
chamber to the garden: two of the windows were filled by
the mountain showing itself as a single expanse of luminous moss or a fleece whose hairs were the trees. I break-
fasted in the room with the wood panelling; nothing here
hinted at the tragedy of the day before. Hélène was
Hélène from up on the mountain: more intense. I would
reconquer her (and the entire memory) through the *bril-
liance* and the *vividness* of these superb things, the splendor of the château on an exceptional morning; I joined
her to the stuccoes, to the severe curtains and to the

precious *substances*; and she was not contradicting my thoughts when she said to me: "In the whole of this house, all I really like is my room; come see it." She took me back into the lofty hallway; to the right of the great room by the entrance was her bedroom.

"This is where I sleep, Léonide." And she opened the door and my eyes fell upon the room.

It was her above all that I saw in the room. Her attitudes were different and superimposed. The Chevelure that morning seemed almost blond. Her body was strong and its flesh gracious. Her mouth smaller and more engaging. Her nostrils quivered and remained immobile. She had taken two anemones from a vase, one white and one red, and kept them between her fingers, twisting them a little. And I, stopped by the recent bereavement but feeling on edge, I struggled not to fall at her feet.

The room was dark blue. The inexpressible nobility of the room derived from its large proportions set round a mass of dark blue velvet, and that mass was the bed. Standing at a distance from the bed were but a very few pieces of furniture, beautiful furniture, placed against the walls. The bed was vast and low, but not enormous; a single person was meant to sleep in it; at each of its four corners the fabric of the baldachin fell straight down, forming a column of velvet, and these four columns with their folds, and the cover, were of the same dark blue. Yet a fair amount of light fell upon the bed; for two windows distributed daylight throughout the room which was hung with a sort of silk or velvet bearing dark blue foliated scrolls against a white background. Of dark blue again, three chairs whose high polished backs rested against the foot of the bed. Three chairs like mute persons; they seemed to be the bed's maid-servants. That dark blue will remain in my memory as long as I am alive.

Following the oriental carpets one came to the adjoining boudoir, ivory in tone and very small with its dream objects probably of lemonwood, and with the low door to the bath, a boudoir so fine it was as though made out of skin, "very fine, very skin," I thought as I lingered there. There, in fact, hung a portrait of a woman with dark eyes, with a gaunt face, not at all pretty, but beautiful, an ancestor of Hélène's, a portrait of the Spanish school; and touching the portrait of this *bitter* woman Hélène said to me: "You're looking at her? She was killed by her husband."

Turning around to her as she uttered these words, I saw her shining from head to foot, young, and I understood the transformation of Hélène that had taken place during the night.

Merely watching her breathe, I was sure of possessing her. I was sure that she would open for me the conch of mysterious life. Our two unconscious bodies would be one single unconscious body. All the pieces of her visible and invisible being, all the reflections, all the intentions, the forms, and the thoughts becoming memories and then words, all became incarnate and intensified under the magic wand. All became more powerful and greater than she. Such a movement of desire toward satisfaction and liberation induced in me an identical desire and movement. I saw my demoniac obsessions "take leave of me." I became simple. The manner I had had of loving her until then (when others were interposed between her and me as advisors or as judges) suddenly repelled me or seemed to me foreign to my nature. A woman superb in verity, consenting but grave, stood before me: was I going to be worthy of her?

XVI

The necessary thing now was no doubt to await friendly or cooperative circumstances, or else to further collect one's thoughts. Desire, too beautiful, bearing too many dark stigmata, still needed *time*.

And why hurry when the goal was so near? Why be so quick to take something that, once taken, would at the very least rob us of *the promise*, the marvellous velleity of things? When I look again with my present eyes at that excruciating state of affairs that existed between Hélène and me, when I think back to the need that state had of all its time—I bless, I bless life that that state of ardent laziness should have existed—and I tremble, seized by terror because it was up to me whether that state might have lasted a good deal longer . . . I kissed the hollow of her hand and the hollows between her fingers. I kissed her mouth and the kiss of her mouth seemed already heaven to me. By my own will I did not go farther, in it checking what I sensed to be frenetic, erectile. Of this continence I was imposing I did not see the meaning, but for it I saw the absolute necessity.

This took place in some one of the rooms on the second floor, for instance in the room where the collections were kept and where the piano stood and where a fire would have been lit in a large stove covered with tiles illustrating a thousand Chinese subjects, and under a single gentle and eternal lamp. The chairs there formed a nook very much withdrawn from the world. I saw among the pieces of ivory and the fans, and on the piano, seven or eight portraits of Hélène at different periods of her life, and almost all these photographs were lovely, adorable, even those with outmoded dresses, and in them Hélène was far more magnificent than her great-grandmother painted by Ribera. Or if I kissed her mouth, it was rather in a small drawing-room that lay on the same floor as the collections room but in the wing opposite her bedroom, a pure marvel: the small room of the children that Hélène had not had! A minuscule place. In it there were books, cameos, a few stuffed birds, miniature Louis XV armchairs. It was here that I loved her the most. At the same time, the pomp of the Château de Ponte had a grating effect on me, I wanted to have Hélène in a hut or a hotel room.

Perhaps she sometimes asked me mutely: what are you waiting for, my beloved, why are you delaying? At these times I would have liked to be able to talk to her about Pauliet. Didn't I owe Pauliet a great deal of my assurance and decision? Wasn't I urged on by him—but restrained by death? "Live, go ahead, go to her! Leap into the abyss . . . As for me, my mother has never left me, and I am dead." I thought I could hear him. But what I thought I had heard would become as if frozen in my mouth when

I tried to convey it to Hélène. Nothing would come forth but a tender and constrained smile. And yet—it really seemed to me that even so she had heard those words! After his mother, whom had he loved most in his whole life? Her.

I still see her. I always see her at that period and at that blessed moment. I don't take my eyes off her. The Promise surrounds us. Oh, there are millions of things that we see and that we do not see. There are a thousand signs! and we are indifferent to the signs. And we are blind once we have understood them and seen them.

XVII

An inhuman, almost unreal tranquillity weighed on the château.

Hélène had dispatched to Sogno, on some errand, the housekeeper who ordinarily slept on the ground floor. The servants who had served us our meal had gone off to bed, since the window of the kitchens in the outbuilding were unlit. The second floor, where lay Monsieur de Sannis's bedroom, with its thick garnet-red baldachin, and the room where I myself slept, dark. In the drawing-room by the entrance, a single lamp had been left on, making fantastic shadows. To be safer I decided against going by way of the hall (the hall with the severe little door) but went through the garden, which lay in complete darkness, into the front drawing-room and from there, through a communicating door that was not closed, into Hélène's bedroom.

The room was blue and empty. It glowed with the special light of the candles.

I would most readily compare the state of expectation in which I found myself to the state of a summer morning. Everything that comprises a man's strength was converging in me but it was freshness with hope. Of my desire, for so long wrought upon and tested, I was by now scarcely aware, so greatly did the truly youthful joy of waiting for her occupy my mind, so well did it cover me with its wings. Most wonderful of all was when I could think "I am yours" and dedicate myself to this woman, who was going to appear through the small door to the boudoir. I stared at that door, I saw it tremble before opening. A strip of light could be seen under it. In the room the large dark blue bed was not prepared for the night, it was still dark blue and the color of profound sensual pleasure. Light proceeding from many sources made for a shadowless brightness and I remembered that there is nothing so gentle to the skin as candlelight. Quickly, I undressed.

Hélène opened the door. She was entirely naked, and had on golden shoes. I clasped my hands before such beauty.

I would never have believed she was so beautiful. I knew her shoulders, I knew her hands well, I did not know them on her naked body. I had always loved the Chevelure but the Chevelure was so much wilder and more lurid resting on the reality of her naked flesh. I did not know her breasts at all: they were rather small, but not far apart, perfectly full and strong, the two fawns of the Song of Songs. I did not know her hips, a little broader than I had dreamed them to be, and I saw for the first time her tuft of hair with its warm color, and lastly, there were her long legs like superb animals, the horses or greyhounds one sees painted in frescoes.

Already I had thrown myself at her. I watched myself do it, with a mind impassive before my avidity I saw myself being so voracious upon her. We rolled together upon the blue bed. Hélène was athletic and totally weak; the violence animating me was, on the contrary, fearful, blind; for, was it not true, in Hélène the gift and the sacrifice were so much richer than my aggression! I saw all these details. Nevertheless, because of her experience, Hélène was able to control my passion, though with difficulty; but she did control it; and that brought her to her triumph: when, engaged in her, I came to the end too quickly. She in her pleasure had taken on an ancient grandeur, her countenance had become worn, her features exaggerated, her eyes had turned inward briefly, after which two large circles had appeared below them, she had not cried out, and everything had subsided in the knowledge of her triumph; her triumph which was in actuality my joy. For after having seen so much, I saw nothing more, I lay surrendered. My joy unfolded after hers, a long time after my pleasure. I had crossed over! I had passed through! I was saved! And this living woman with the body of a queen belonged to me! And my pleasure, my joy came back to me after the thing was past and I relived a hundred times more joyful and voluptuous the thing itself that I had done. Toward the end I had raised my arm in the air like a flag, I remembered; I said this to her, and she: "Yes, you raised your arm, and your fingers made the sign of reaching something, and your clinging hand was the most splendid there could be under the sun." She covered me with passionate kisses and I had the right to these kisses and I returned them all. I fell asleep on her. When I woke up it was broad day and I was lying in my own room.

I might have believed I had been dreaming. But there was a piece of paper under the door, I opened the envelope, which bore no name, the note was from Hélène. "I am happy happy happy! The world is not big enough for my happiness." Everything came back: my strength, my consciousness of myself, my glory. But how had I come to be here? I got dressed. I met Hélène in the second floor parlor. What a tender goddess. (The tender distance, which was necessary, already caused us to suffer.) I recall that outside, snow was falling. Hélène against this great background of eternal whiteness was the representation of summer, the promise of eternal heat. She smiled at me with such an infinite art of secrecy that I did not even dare question her, but it was she who said to me, as soon as we were alone, and after we had embraced each other, that I had regained my room half carried by her, between lucidity and sleep. I remembered nothing.

Thus had she profoundly transformed my being. Over and done with was my self-criticism, precise and crushing. Through love, in Hélène and through Hélène, I thought, I was approaching inevitable and fecund unreason; I was within reach of the remote and cloudy beginnings, of the fountain-head which is that of the Mothers. The pride of the moult must be dazzling in an animal: I was experiencing it. I was experiencing it to the highest degree, because for the first time in my life I was happy, sure of my flesh and of my consciousness, through a self that had emerged and freed itself of the "I alone."

. . . No doubt, instead of drifting with the current of

my happiness, I ought to have thought more about the mysterious woman, noticed the traces of a slight and melancholy fatigue on the admirable face that snowy morning, better surrounded her, defended her . . . That morning, which was the first of my life as a man, I was mindful only of living. Yet just then, I thought again of the Woman in Black whom I had once seen, so beautiful and so menacing. I drove away the dream! I made it be still! I would no longer have there be a Woman in Black since here was Hélène de Sannis, illuminated by our night, resplendant against the snow.

XVIII

She kept the door of her room closed during the nights that followed. I examine myself. I inspect myself at that crucial time to determine all my responsibilities. I find in myself the wild contradictions of happiness. Thus I had physically and in all reality enacted that paramount scene, I had had it, with her—and because of what she was, of what she had always been, this violation once committed, I was deeply upset by what I had done, and *supremely happy to have done it!* Visions assailed me; for instance I saw Madame de Sannis again walking in the meadow at noon amid the harmonies of summer. I greeted Madame de Sannis once again, my hand pompously raised to my cap. I took Madame de Sannis there and I placed her over Hélène here. I trembled from head to toe during this mental operation. It was joy! But the idea of violation and of incest were not separate from it. The effect of this was that I took my adoration of her still farther back. Thus, once again I spoke to her "for the first time" by the Torre church with a warm and guilty heart, intoxicated by her sovereign appearances, which were those of the inaccessible *grande dame*. And now, and now. The marvellous, deep blue skies of the meadow and of Torre descended once again into my heart, filled my chest, as if I had had them and conquered them. Certain shameful little scenes between the period of the Torre sky and the period of the victory on the blue bed now seemed to me without importance and without beauty alike. Pauliet's shade was also a shadow cast aslant things, come here for no other reason than to assist in the greatest love of my existence. And finally in my burning selfishness a sort of waning occurred, and in my thoughts I sank down to my knees before her.

I wanted as well to flee from her. Oh, merely in order to find her again afterwards and chain myself to her the more powerfully with our chains. What unnamed Power was there, whose hand, whose influence I sensed? For I was also experiencing a vague religious terror: what would happen if we were to go to the very end? The end between the two of us had not yet been reached—and this end, of a terrible violence and richness—how were we to endure it? World too high, world too strong—to be human. So it was no longer the past that made me ashamed and that I had had the joy of conquering; it was the future that frightened me because, for it, the substance I had would not be inexhaustible enough. Hélène was indeed my woman: but how to make my life with her life!

And when I contemplated her privately, I thought: I have her. *Nothing* could ever weaken that reality. What other woman would have professed with such vehemence that the time of the Promise was no longer, that the very heaven was exceeding itself, and that she accepted that excess with all her soul and wanted it to be exceeded, that Torre sky, always farther and more. If she had deigned to speak, she would have expressed in this way her divine disappointment, she would have said: "that the time of the Promise was the true time and that she had always known this; that she knew it well, and that she was awaiting further kisses."

XIX

She said to me at nightfall:

"Come tonight, and I will give myself to you, this time."

Everything was prepared, as on the first night, in a dazzlingly festive atmosphere. It was she who was waiting for me when I entered in the candlelight. There were many candles.

Hélène was otherwise arrayed. She was wearing a long silk dress, its sleeves of a light color, that opened down the front of her body. The thin dress fell like a peplos. But on her feet she still wore the golden shoes. I was confused at not finding her the same. At feeling her to be more imposing. I knelt up against her and I lay my head to her belly.

When I think of myself taking that position and of how long I remained in it.

Our fury began. Hélène was of a strength so direct and so exciting, and in what she did was of a virtue so profound, at the same time so ingenious and so skilled in sensual pleasure, that at once my young strength developed prodigiously, and it became a battle between us, a long battle with pauses, resumptions, exultations and sobs. Hélène knew everything; there was not a harmonic of the body that she did not know how to awaken, and not a groan that did not rise from her heart. Inventions, sometimes perverse games were conducted by her with a thrilling liveliness, strained with dizzying intensity toward the end at which her wide-open tear-filled eyes did not cease to gaze. I do not know how much time this long labor of our indistinct bodies lasted, this concluding of their love in knowledge. But I was the first to be overtaken by pleasure, like a whirlwind. She followed me that same instant. This was Pleasure. It is the abyss—the abyss Pauliet spoke of—, this was what I was thinking with the bit of intelligence that had been preserved apart. The abyss opened with such frenzy and with such an orgy of abyss, and I was led to it by such joy, or such woe, that it was with indifference that I heard Hélène cry out, utter a plaintive little cry. Soon the abyss moved away, the bed and the other things reappeared, I regained my senses and immediately remembered that she had cried out. I clasped her again. Her head was turned to one side, and as I sank into a state of torpor I was aware that she was moving and that she was leaving me.

Hélène had gone off for a moment. I was dozing on the bed. But there she was again. She was coming back. She lay down on the bed next to me, naked in her long antique and maternal dress. Hélène had come back in order to go to sleep. Stretched out on the bed, her eyes were shining with gratitude to God, and I was saying tender things to her, when . . . her eyes under her loosened

Chevelure at first grew dim, it looked as though a veil were covering them. Then she regained her sight, but became extremely pale. Her pallor increased. I demanded of her: "Hélène, Hélène! You must be having a dizzy spell. Speak to me." Smiling, with admirable composure, she motioned to me to go into the boudoir and she said "Ether." A brief inhalation of ether did her good, she smiled again as if to apologize, and revived right away. As for me, however, anguish seized my heart as though in a vise that did not loosen, as though the improvement that had followed could not fool me. We remained thus, I on my knees in front of her. The smell of ether filled the room, which had for so long been full of burning smells.

Hélène was growing paler. I saw that her hands and feet were cold. What was I to do for her? I kissed her. The idea of scandal was there before my eyes, preventing me from calling for help. What was more, she was gesturing to me not to call, and then she told me fiercely: "Don't call anyone." I rubbed her hands and feet, her chest, I patted her temples with eau de Cologne, and I kissed the Chevelure, entreating it to act in our favor, for the Chevelure had the power that works miracles. It was all too plain that something serious was happening somewhere inside her and that her silence, her gentleness, were covering her frightful awareness of this. With her two clenched hands she wrapped the silk dress around her body, still looking at me. Her eyes were shining now with a very strong light. I did nothing but embrace her, for everything was going so fast that it was impossible to do anything. But Hélène opened her mouth, spoke, reassured me. She reassured me: "It's easy . . . Easy . . . It's easy to die. I swear to you. Don't fret . . . Easy . . ." Her speech was so clear, so like her. Twice she said "Léonide," and after the second: "Léonide, be happy." And she went on with a more extreme gentleness: "It's easy . . . It's beautiful and easy with you . . ." Tears blinding me, I could no longer see her. She said also: Pray with me. I heard her reciting in a low voice "Our Father who art in heaven." Once more she turned her whole face to me, her whole living face, said: "I . . . love you, I thank you," or "My love I thank you," I could not make it out.

She became completely white. Her breath left her.

I threw myself upon her with a horrible clumsiness. I rubbed her body, all of it; I put the wad of ether against her nostrils; I slapped her, I called her by her name. Her eyes were hidden behind her eyelids. Silent. Before me now I had only the pale thing. Her heart. Her heart! How could I revive her heart. In the dressing table there was a syringe, I filled it with ether and injected it into her. *Her heart*. Her heart had caused her to die. I repeated: her heart. She died because of her heart.

I shouted out that it was impossible! Despite myself I began praying for her. Old, forgotten prayers came back intact to my memory. I recited over her the entire *De Profundis*.

But not believing she was dead I put my head on her breast to listen to her heart. There was silence. And I took a small mirror, I placed it and placed it again in front of her mouth. Here also the absence was complete. No blur, nothing. Silence! Silence! A minute before, when she was in the throes of death—when she was still alive—I believed I would die with her. Now, I did not

94

even think of killing myself, to such an extent was my will composed of her, her still alive, and the continuation of her.

She slept with an extreme gentleness.

I prayed for another hour. She had remained naked after the attempts I had made to chafe her. I piously covered her with her silk dress, and because the thought of scandal now stayed with me, I arranged the scene as was necessary. I left her hands loose. I covered her with the sheet up to her chest. She appeared to be lying in her bed, in a certain disorder. I put her golden shoes away. I left the flask of ether uncorked with the wad, but I carried away the syringe in my pocket. The silent crash of horror fell around me.

XX

My life—in those first moments—had only one idea: to wrest her from death, to carry her off, dead, from death, to force her to revive somewhere, in me, in us, to resuscitate her, by force, by means of a *concentration of myself*. She was perhaps dead for others; not for me. She was not dead—for me—at the moment when we entered together and one by way of the other into the absolute of existence. If she was dead at that moment, dead from love, I was dead too. Was I dead, then? I was not dead, therefore she "was not dead." This singular logic did its own work beyond my will, and I think that its true role was to allow the pain to act. I searched for the means by which she would not be dead for the two of us, even if others would have to find her dead and carry her away as dead: for it mattered little what they did if I myself managed to make it so that she was not dead.

However, this delirium I had flung myself into yielded suddenly at the proper moment so that I could pass into the personality of another man, who forgot nothing of all that he had to accomplish so that that there would not be any scandal surrounding Hélène, so that everything would be the way she wanted it, the way it should be. The contradiction led to the notion of *a woman not truly dead, a counterfeit dead woman*, a particularly frightful thought, a thought that dictated imperious duties to me, gave me skill, awoke an amazing energy, in short made me live. I acted then the way mad people do. Had it been necessary, I would have taken her around the waist and transported her from one place to another. For two or three hours I experienced the *calmest*, the most powerfully calm time in my entire life. All of this was conditional upon her being a "counterfeit dead woman."

I will not give all the details. The people of the house and the neighborhood were gathered around Hélène— "whom I had heard crying out in the middle of the night"—when I hurried out to get the doctor from the village. I brought back this doctor, a very old man who had seen Hélène as a child, and who, sensing she was in danger, was almost weeping as he ran with me. All of a sudden with an extraordinary lucidity (but still convinced that I was talking about a not truly dead woman) I stopped him under a tree in the courtyard before the house, and, touching his arm with my hand, which was trembling convulsively, I said to him: "I was with Madame de Sannis, in her room, when the heart failure occurred. Do you understand what I mean?" He did not answer right away. He stared at me in the shadow, I who appeared as unhinged as anyone could. I was preventing him from moving. Immediately he said: "I understand, sir." We continued on our way. I thought I had to give him an explanation: "I love Madame de Sannis."

I no longer had much control over my words.

Later, in my room, I began to sleep. I woke up shrieking. I could hear distinctly: "My little lion . . . my little lion . . ." and the voice, her voice, persisted, remained there through a perpetual echo: "My little lion . . ."

From the *nonexistent* sound of that voice I understood that she was no longer. In the words "My little lion . . ." which came to me from such a formidable distance, I abruptly discovered reality. I saw that she was dead— dead for herself—dead for me. She was dead; there was no more of her, there never would be more of her, she would never more be, in the sense in which I still was, in all of eternity she would never again belong to me. A prolonged cry of terror went through me and as I uttered it I lost consciousness; for I returned to myself an hour later faced with the same thoughts, alone in the world, unable to move my arms or legs. I had uttered my cry of terror in the presence of that *never more*, now it expanded into a flood of tears and more tears, but I cried out again every time I discovered another aspect of the reality: for example when I thought of the proximity in time of that pleasure and that death; for example when I pictured to myself what she *became* at that moment, a few feet away from me, in the light of the tapers. I was not yet able to succeed in grasping the link, in what had happened, between the kiss of kisses that had triumphantly passed through all the obstacles of life itself, and the *opposite* of the kiss—her, dead. I was no longer able to understand either life or death. I confused them. Yet it did not occur to my feelings to continue to desire her, dead. No, death had projected her into death which was my Enemy. Where was she? I did not dare to think. But in order not to touch death with a sacrilegious hand, I said that now she was nowhere, that now she was *nothing* in my life and in my love. At that point, therefore, the horror was not the worst thing; the worst thing was the *asphyxia* that followed my complete privation. The air was withdrawn from my being. It was forbidden to live the minute following this one, since in the minute, in every minute, what was essential to life had been snatched away. There is no more atrocious feeling for a living being than this one: when in the fullness of life he sees his life cut off from outside. Hélène, in dying, had cut off my life. Physically, even, I was no longer managing to get air to move through my throat, I thought I was turning blue, there is no way to describe the torture in which I panted. I have lost everything: my lover, my mother, my sister, the source itself, woman. I have lost my heart swollen with blood. I have lost my breath. I have lost my spirit . . .

The night, the paramount night of my existence, rolled over me and came to its end.

At dawn, however, I had a revelation. Was it she who, from some inexpressible place, was acting, influencing my soul? At the time, the shock being so sudden, I believed this; *I wanted to believe it.* "When the most stricken being can no longer make a single movement, he must accept." Such was the phrase in my luminous thought. The most stricken being is in the presence of the creator of his spirit: therefore he must *accept.* At the same time that I was thinking, I was able to stand up and cross the room and descend the stairs and reach the door of Hélène's room, open the door. A dark light, from yellow tapers, rested gently on her, long, elongated as it seemed to me, with a face seized by a perfect peace, a perfect joy. Only the Chevelure recalled life a little, reddening under the glow of the taper. A mystical fragrance already made her more majestic. I understood something infinite. I no longer recognized the room, in it I was a stranger. Two nuns on their knees, on either side of the bed, were reciting prayers, and there was someone else sitting in the shadow, but my presence was completely unnoticed. I kneeled down too, in order to look at her one more time. Yes, there appeared in me an extraordinary power. Yes, a mysterious and simple work was being done. I no longer doubted the omnipotence of her soul. How, I did not know. But she began to live as a soul, I was sure of it. And never, since the first hour, had I adored her as I did seeing her dead. I spent a long time close to her. Nothing changed, nothing separated itself out in the edifice of my prayer. Hélène's repose was, in my faith which had at last accepted it, sublime, and creative. Later I shivered . . .

Someone came up to me and led me back to my room.

XXI

What had come about within me did not give me the power to follow Hélène's coffin. For nights and days on end my heartbreak grew unendingly worse, without, at the point where I was, causing me further pain. Confined to my bed, I had a nervous fever accompanied by delirium. In an immense subterranean labor I mingled thoughts and dreams. It was given to me to be able to picture, through everything that had happened, happiness and unhappiness, in darkness or in light, the destiny of that wonderful woman. Once again I saw the Meadow, the Chevelure, my Sogno anguishes, my perversities, Pauliet appeared, with a sepulchral face, more truly *dead*, Pauliet who had caused death to appear; but I always came back to Destiny, to Hélène's secret, to her destiny making fertile my destiny. I believed I could glimpse, catch by surprise, several women, see them detach themselves from Hélène and blend back into her, like different layers of her, the ones more remote in time than the others. All these women profounder than Hélène, and who were Hélène, came together in the Woman in Black whom I had seen in a dream. I felt essentially that for me (somewhere in me where resemblance among figures is not necessary) Hélène had always been identical with the Woman in Black, and the Woman in Black worshipped as Hélène. The Woman in Black whom I had seen was the anticipation of Hélène: the one in an unfortunate marriage, the one who was going to die. Oh, was there not something else? All the confusion, all the tears in these images! But it was clear (this I had *known*) that Hélène's first role was to have brought me into the world; being the mother of my heart, to have changed herself into the mistress of my heart. Being the age of the mother, to have given herself as though to the son. Was this woman in black not the terrible maternal woman, whom I had to take, whom I had taken in triumph? Oh, there was yet more and more still! As though this Woman in Black were a piece of my flesh. As though the desperate one, the woman who bursts out laughing, she who must flee into unhappiness, *was myself*, the very mystery of myself, the part that Hélène had allowed me to *espouse*; as though, for the salvation of this woman in black whom she had divined, predestined to flight, Hélène had sacrificed her life.

In the intuition of this, I sat up in my bed. I stared into eternity at: Hélène, and behind her and in her the conquered Woman in Black; I made a vow to consecrate to the image of the Woman in Black, in Hélène's memory, the store of strengths I could feel nearing birth.

For through this remembrance, something that I could not yet name was beginning to be born. By way of the thread of remembrance and evocation, through the movement of love that adhered to them, through the might of the trembling of terror and of the yearning that surrounded it, I felt confused things recreating themselves, things which sought a name, names, which from the interior of thought were going to find their magic names and rush forth into the outside. Certain states—of melancholy, joy, annunciation, despair—false states compared to the world of pain and solitude, but more real than the world and saved by an intimate spark, the only states which allowed me to communicate with Hélène henceforth, to rediscover Hélène gentle and black henceforth, these states occurred now for me, came close to me, left me, came back. It was a flight of nocturnal birds lighter-hued than the birds of the daytime. I wanted to capture the states that did me so much good, write them down on paper. Alas, I did not know the signs, or what required capturing. I did not succeed in doing it. But a patience, new and deep, was also forming . . .

I saw Monsieur de Sannis again, as courtesy demanded.

I went away from the Château de Ponte without turning my head. There—I knew it later—a perfect, that is to say an inexhaustible spring had opened for me.

I left without visiting the grave.